Seeing Lessons

Seeing Lessons

Maria

Charles

Benjamin

Joseph/Young Joe

‹✿ SPRING HERMANN
with illustrations by IB OHLSSON

The Story of Abigail Carter and
America's First School for Blind People

Sophia   *Abby*

Henry Holt and Company · New York

Henry Holt and Company, Inc., *Publishers since 1866*
115 West 18th Street, New York, New York 10011

Henry Holt is a registered trademark of Henry Holt and Company, Inc.

Published in Canada by Fitzhenry & Whiteside Ltd.,
195 Allstate Parkway, Markham, Ontario L3R 4T8.

Library of Congress Cataloging-in-Publication Data
Hermann, Spring.
Seeing Lessons: the story of Abigail Carter and America's first school
for blind people / Spring Hermann; with illustrations by Ib Ohlsson.
p.   cm.
Summary: When ten-year-old Abby Carter attends the newly
established school for the blind in Boston in 1832, she proves that blind
people can learn and be independent.
1. Carter, Abigail, d. 1875—Juvenile fiction.   [1. Carter, Abigail, d. 1875—Fiction.
2. Blind—Fiction. 3. Physically handicapped—Fiction. 4. Schools—Fiction.]
I. Ohlsson, Ib, ill. II. Title. PZ7.H43167Se 1998 [Fic]—dc21   97-42570

ISBN 0-8050-5706-4
First Edition—1998   Designed by Nicole Stanco
Printed in the United States of America on acid-free paper. ∞
1 3 5 7 9 10 8 6 4 2

For Vincent, Rosalie, and Norman—
three of my best fans

❧   ❧   ❧

My thanks and appreciation go to the following institutions, whose staffs assisted immeasurably in researching this book: the Andover Historical Society, Andover, Massachusetts; Central Connecticut State University Library; the Houghton Library, Harvard University; the Massachusetts Historical Society, Boston, Massachusetts; and the Reference Library of the Perkins School for the Blind, Watertown, Massachusetts.

I also wish to thank the Society of Children's Book Writers and Illustrators for awarding me a work-in-progress grant to assist in funding my research.

CONTENTS

Preface

Suppose you were a blind child growing up in America in the 1820s. Suppose you wanted to go to school and get an education so you could get a good job. You could not follow this dream in America. No schools for the blind existed. It was believed that blind people should stay home and be protected by their families.

A medical student from Boston, John Fisher, was studying in Paris, France, during the 1820s. He discovered an amazing school, the National Institution for Blind Youth. When Dr. Fisher went home to Boston to practice medicine, he told his friends about the blind pupils he saw in Paris. They decided to start such a school in Boston. The Massachusetts legislature granted a charter on March 2, 1829. They called their school the New England Asylum for the Blind. *Asylum* then meant a sheltered place to live and work.

Who would be in charge of this school? Dr. Fisher and the thirty-eight other Boston men who signed up as "incorporators" of the school wanted just the right person. After having a meeting, Dr. Fisher and several of the incorporators walked down the street. They bumped into a friend of Fisher's who was also known to the others: Dr. Samuel Gridley Howe.

Fisher shouted, "Here is Howe! The very man we have been looking for!"

Dr. Howe was twenty-nine years old in the spring of 1831 when he was asked to become the first director of the planned school. He had studied only surgery. He was a bachelor with no children and little money. He knew no blind people. Still, Dr. Howe believed he was the perfect man for the job. The incorporators sent Dr. Howe to Paris to study the way that school was run. He went on to Germany, England, Scotland, and Belgium to study schools for the blind there. He found much to admire. He also improved many things.

When Dr. Howe sailed home to Boston, he brought with him two blind teachers. Pringle from Scotland and Trencheri from France would not only teach. They would show Americans that blind people could be independent and handle any job.

Dr. Howe needed only two more things: money to run the school and pupils. Dr. Fisher had written to the Congregational churches in Massachusetts. He asked if any blind children lived in their towns. Many church pastors replied yes. The first ones on the list came from the congregation of Andover, Massachusetts: Abigail Carter and her younger sister, Sophia. Knowing he had no money, Dr. Howe still set out to convince parents a school for the blind would start.

With faith and hope in his heart, Dr. Howe drove up to the tollhouse at Andover. There, as he arrived, stood Abigail and Sophia Carter.

It was a lucky accident that Abby Carter was the first blind child on Dr. Howe's list. It was pure chance that she stood at the tollhouse as he drove up. The luckiest person on that day, however, was not Dr. Howe. It was Abby Carter. Before that day, she thought she would spend her life doing chores on the family farm. She never even dreamed of an education or a career. For the rest of her life, she told everybody that she owed every achievement and success to lessons she learned from Dr. Howe and his school.

This is the story of Abby Carter, her sister Sophia, and their teacher Dr. Samuel Howe. It is also the story of their fellow pupils, Ben, Maria, Charles, and Joe; the Carter family; the Howe family; and friends. All the people in this story really lived their lives much as it is written here. We can't know exactly what these people said to each other or what their hopes and fears and dreams were. We can only know what they did. We can use letters, journals, school reports, memoirs, articles, and stories told to us by people who watched Abby and the school grow. For the rest of the story, we must use our imagination.

Seeing Lessons

Dr. Fisher

Dr. Howe

❧ 1
The Magic Road

"Abbee!"

My little brother, Edward, was bawling because he was getting left behind us.

"Hurry up," I told my sister, Sophia. "Let the boys tend Edward for a change."

Sophia groped for my hand. "Don't run off without me, Abby."

Through my slippers, my toes searched for the soft dirt. I followed the ruts and turns of our land. The slant of the morning sun hit my left cheek. The scent of our cow pen drifted from the right. I drew the picture in my head to lead me on.

"Are we coming to the pike?" Sophia asked. "Can you hear any horses?"

"We're not close enough yet. Mind your steps."

I'd been leading Sophia down to the Essex Turn-pike for years. She still dreaded tumbling off the road-side bluff. If she landed in the road, she might get kicked by a buggy horse. We had an older brother who got mule kicked and died. Sophia feared the same fate.

Sophia didn't trust the pictures in her head. I was ten, and she was only six. Yet at her age, I could find my way all over the farm. Soph was not so daring. She had a terror of getting lost.

To me, the Essex Turnpike was the magic road to everyplace. It came from north of our town of Andover and ran along the edge of our fields. If you rode it all the way to the end, you landed in Boston. At the end of our path sat the tollhouse. Here folks paid their fees to ride the pike.

"Hey, Abby. Hey, Sophia."

I smiled at the familiar voice of Mr. Holt, the toll man. He spent his days in the little house and allowed us to sit by his doorway.

"Hey, Mr. Holt. How do y'do today?" I asked.

"Right well, girls. Come sit on my bench."

I led Sophia along the roadside and sat her down. "What travelers have come by today?"

"A stage from Lowell. Three fine-dressed ladies with feathers on their bonnets. Two farm wagons loaded with vegetables. And your pastor came by in his gig."

"Fine-dressed ladies? What did they talk about?" I asked.

"Now, Abby, I can't be listening in on folks when I take the toll," he said.

"We listen in," Sophia said. "That's how we find out what's happening."

"That's so, poor blind thing. And no one can fault you."

I sniffed and listened and touched my toes to the ground. A dusty scent? A soft thunder? A tremble in the earth? "Mr. Holt," I said in a hush, "someone's coming from the south."

"Lordy, Miss Abby, you're the keen one."

Sophia and I leaned forward on the bench. The excitement grew inside me. The far-off crack of a driver's whip cut the air as the horse came hard and fast. When the hoofbeats were near upon us, they pounded like a second heart in my chest. Road dust on the breeze filled my nose, along with the smell of horse sweat. Then the driver curbed his horse.

"Morning to ye, gentlemen," Mr. Holt called out.

"Good morning," said the driver. "We are in need of some directions."

"That'll be a quarter for your buggy. Heading north?"

I stood up to hear the driver's deep voice. Sophia, holding my hand, got up too.

"Good morning, girls," the driver said.

"Morning," I said, and dropped a curtsy. I felt Sophia press her face against my sleeve. She was seized with a shyness from being with strange men.

"Them's the Carter girls," Mr. Holt said. "They like to hear about those that travel the pike. They got a young brother, blind like them."

Sophia and I were used to folks talking about our blindness. Another man in the buggy called to the driver, "By the good Lord, Howe. Isn't this extraordinary?"

Extra-ordinary? I liked to learn new long words.

"Yes," the driver agreed. "Here stand our children. The very ones we have come to enlist. Just waiting for Providence to enter their lives."

Providence? Our pastor talked about Providence. I never figured out exactly what it meant. Even in the sun, I felt a shiver.

The other man from the buggy came over to us and gently patted my head. He smelled like a city man, all fine leather wear and wintergreen and none of the barn.

"Don't worry, girls," he said. "I am Doctor Fisher, and this is Doctor Howe. We came from Boston."

The man put a tiny hard ball into my palm. "Will

TOLL
Charges:

HORSE & WAGON
COWS
PIGS
SHEEP

you girls tell me your names? And take a sweet from me?"

"Yes, sir," I said. Real doctors all the way from Boston? "My name is Abigail Carter. This here's Sophia."

Soph got so nervous, she started to squeeze me. "Put your hand out," I said. "You'll get a sweet."

Sophia swallowed hard. "You get one for me?"

Doctor Howe stooped so his voice came at our height. "I'm pleased to meet you, Abigail and Sophia. Would you do Doctor Fisher and me a great favor? We have come to speak to your parents. Please guide us back to your house."

"Our parents?" I asked. "There's nobody sick at our place."

Doctor Fisher said, "That's fine, but we have important business there."

I was amazed but remembered my manners. "Follow me, please. Good day to you, Mr. Holt." I led Sophia back up the path, showing the doctors the road. As we walked, I heard Doctor Howe driving the horse. I got so churned up at being the leader that I rushed along. Sophia lost her footing and fell flat on her belly. She cried from shame as she picked herself up.

"Abbeee! You pulled me too fast!"

"I'm sorry. Don't cry in front of strangers."

When I reached out for the rail fence that turns up toward the house, it wasn't there.

Sophia said, "We aren't far enough past the stony place."

"I know," I mumbled, embarrassed to forget my own way. Fences don't fly just because you can't see them. After another reach, I touched it.

"I'll settle the doctors in the parlor," I told her as we neared the front door. "Find Mam in the kitchen. Papa and the boys are working in the barn."

"What'd that doctor mean, important business?" Sophia asked.

"How would I know? Run off now," I said.

As Sophia went to find Mam, I called to the gentlemen, "Please to tie your horse here. My brothers will come water him."

The doctors did so, then followed me into our parlor. Mam had her two fine carved chairs there and a settee. Papa's writing table with his books stood by the iron stove on the hearth. The parlor with its closed drapes stayed cool in summer.

"Please to sit on our good chairs," I said. Then I fell silent. I heard Papa with the boys stomp into the kitchen. A nagging thought popped right out of my mouth:

"Doctor Howe, you said about Providence coming? And important business here? Did you mean with me and Sophia?"

Doctor Howe replied, "Yes. You are the ones we seek."

I felt excited and confused and scared all at once. How could I have guessed that? Then I heard Mam call to me. "I have to help my mother," I said, and hurried back to the kitchen.

"Abby," Mam said, "what's this Sophia says about strangers?"

"Yes! In the parlor. Papa had better go."

Edward was squirming and fussing. Mam was trying to contain him. "You did a fairly poor job on those snap beans, my girls," Mam said. "You know how I depend on you."

"Yes, Mam," I said, "but those strangers have real important business. And it's—"

"Your business is doing chores for your family, miss. Now keep Edward from fussing while I tend to the gentlemen."

We could hear Papa greeting the doctors and introducing our big brothers. Soon Mam brought them luncheon plates and cold tea. I'd never been so curious in my life. Two Boston doctors drove right up the magic toll road and into our lives. Whatever might happen to us next?

2

Doctor and His Dream

Mam made Sophia and me sit on the floor by the stove and amuse Edward. After she served the gentlemen, I heard them exclaim how fine a luncheon she gave them. We girls were itching with impatience. Why were we "important business"? Doctor Howe said he'd like to tell us all a story. Papa said that would be fine. Doctor Howe took a swallow of his tea and set his spoon onto the plate with a little clink. He cleared his throat.

"Last year I came back to Boston, to my father's home. I had worked and studied many years in foreign lands as a surgeon. Somewhere along the way I had lost my love of surgery. You may think that seeing people never get lost, but I was feeling lost myself."

11

Sophia poked me as if to say, How could that be?

"One day my friend Doctor Fisher saw me standing on the street corner. He said I looked like I was waiting for Providence to enter my life."

I poked Sophia back as if to say, He was waiting just like we were?

"I'd been searching for a new path," said Doctor Howe. "Suddenly Fisher shouted, 'Here you are! The very man I have been seeking!'"

We heard Doctor Fisher chuckle at that. "I must explain," he said. "Years ago, when I studied medicine in Paris, I saw a wonderful school there. I wanted to start such a special school in Boston. All we needed was the right director. I knew in an instant that day I saw Howe—he was the man!"

"Fisher and his friends raised money to send me across the ocean to France and Scotland," Doctor Howe said. "There I saw the most extraordinary things. Children were reading books, writing stories, solving math problems, playing instruments, and making handicrafts. Why was that extraordinary, Abigail?"

"Oh! I don't know. What is extra-ordinary?"

"It means something you would never expect. The extraordinary thing about it was that those children were blind."

"Blind!" I blurted. "How could they read if they couldn't see the book? How could they write if they couldn't see the pen or the paper?"

"Hush, Abby," said Papa, "don't talk out of turn."

"Sorry," I said.

"I could not believe it myself," said Doctor Howe. "Yet they were blind. Most of their teachers were blind also. When I returned to Boston, I said to Doctor Fisher, we must do for our blind children what they are doing in France and Scotland. And because we are clever Yankees, we must do it better!"

Doctor Fisher chuckled again. "That's why we gave Howe the job. He thinks nothing is impossible for a Yankee."

"We have started a school for the blind in Boston," said Doctor Howe. "It was put on paper almost four years ago. Here it is, 1832, and we are finally ready to get started. We want Abigail and Sophia to be our first pupils."

Doctor Howe stayed quiet while we swallowed our surprise. Edward, who was only three, deviled the cat. Richard snorted in disbelief to Justin. Sophia grabbed my arm and giggled. A school? *For us?* My stomach grew lively like a bag of frogs.

Papa spoke slow and soft. "This is quite a notion, Doctors. I expect you mean well. But it is a sin to get Mrs. Carter's hopes up. She has known such sorrow with the children."

"Mr. Carter, please trust me," Doctor Howe said. "Let me have charge of the girls for one year. I'll treat them with the same care I would lavish on my own daughters. Doctor Fisher will look after their health. And you will have no expense. Just deliver them and supply their clothing. What do you say?"

"Sir, this is mighty hard to believe. We do depend on Abby for chores around the farm. Little Edward needs tending. And another child is due in the fall. So . . ."

"Mr. Carter. Doctors. May I speak?"

It was Mam. I expect Papa nodded yes, because Doctor Howe said, "Of course, Mrs. Carter."

"Our boys here, Richard and Justin, can see fairly well. But one boy not here is Gilbert. He was blind as a baby, just like the girls and Edward. We lost him because he got his head kicked by a mule. A farm is a hard place to be blind. A blind child must be quicker and smarter than a seeing one."

A deep sadness came into Mam's voice when she talked about Gilbert. I still remembered him and missed him. Then she took a long breath.

"It's the Lord's will that we lost a child. Many others have this cross to bear. But the girls can do mighty well when they keep their minds on their duties. I believe they are smart as any other children. I will do without my girls if you give them a chance to show just how smart they are."

That was a long speech for Mam, who always let Papa do the talking with visitors. I put my arm around

Sophia and gave her a quick hug. We'd seldom heard Mam praise us so.

"Mrs. Carter," said Doctor Howe, "I am a bachelor. I can't know the great love a parent has for a child. But I can tell you this: I will fight for your children. They will receive the same respect a seeing child gets. No one will doubt them ever again."

Papa said to Doctor Howe, "Boston's a mighty big city. Where would you be keeping my girls?"

The doctor paused and sounded like he was sipping his tea and thinking what to say.

Sophia whispered in my ear, "Boston! I'm scared I'll get lost so far from home."

"Hush, now," I whispered back, and gave her a tiny shove. Boston was down the Essex Turnpike! I'd always dreamed of traveling. This could be my chance.

"Your daughters," Doctor Howe said slowly, "would be kept in my father's home. My sisters will help me. There will be room for about six students. They will be taught by gentlemen from the blind schools in France and Scotland."

"No schoolhouse?" Papa asked. "Lessons in the parlor?"

"At first," Doctor Howe replied. "Our legislators don't understand that blind pupils can learn. But your daughters will convince them. And the state will grant money to purchase a school building."

"So . . ." Papa spoke slowly. "This business may be riding on my girls?"

"That's so," Doctor Howe replied. "I believe Providence has brought us together."

"Well, Abigail?" Papa called on me with my proper name. "Would you work hard for the doctor so as not to disgrace him?"

"Oh, I would, ever so hard, Papa. I want to learn."

"And you, Sophia. Would you study with your sister?"

"I won't stay behind without her," Sophia said. "Even though she pinches me sometimes."

"Soph! The doctor won't take us if he thinks we're scrappy."

Doctor Howe chuckled. "You and Abby will be so busy that you'll have little time for quarrels."

"Then, Doctors," said Papa, "I'll bring the girls to you."

"Excellent!" said Doctor Howe. "I'll put down the directions to my house in Boston. On September first, we shall start school."

"We must go now," said Doctor Fisher. "We have a few more pupils to meet in other towns."

"Blind like us?" Sophia asked.

"Yes," Doctor Howe said. "There are many like you in Massachusetts. But you are the very first pupils chosen. You must lead the way."

"Abby can do it," Sophia said. "She leads me and Edward all over the farm."

"I knew that the moment I saw her," Doctor Howe said.

When I felt his faith in me, goose bumps ran down my arms. He made me believe in myself and my learning. Suddenly it was done. Papa shook hands on it with the doctors. I was going to school. The idea was so big, I couldn't stuff it into my head.

Later, when the doctors called good-bye and headed for the turnpike, their voices kept dancing in my ears. The dream that they gave to us had so many parts. I tried to piece the dream together like a patchwork, but it was too hard.

That evening we children walked down the path behind the house to the privy. Sophia and I went ahead. Richard was trying to keep his hand on Edward, who was supposed to be doing his toilet like a big boy. Edward still forgot sometimes about keeping his britches dry.

"Edward," I called to him. "You better grow up this summer and behave. Because Sophia and I are going off to school. We can't be tending to you." It was silly to tell Edward about going off to school. Yet I liked to hear the words spoken.

"Richard," Sophia said, "we go to Boston on September first. How many days is it until then?"

Richard said, "About four weeks in June and four in July and four in August. That's twelve weeks. But there's seven days in a week. I wish I had my slate to get that number."

"You get numbers off your slate in school? Will we do that?" I asked.

"Edward, get busy in the privy," Richard said. Then he told me, "You write your numbers on a slate while you're working on them in your head. So maybe this doctor will find some kind of magic slate? That blind people can see?" That made him chuckle.

"Richard!" I snapped. "Are you poking fun at the doctor?"

"Guess so. 'Cause how he can teach you things you can't see, I can't figure."

"Maybe there *is* a magic slate," I said. "You don't know everything, Richard. If those blind children across the sea can learn numbers, so can we. We'll learn all that you know!"

"Oh, ho, listen to you, Abby." Richard laughed again. Then he quit his teasing and got Edward off the privy. But if my own brother was laughing at this dream of a school, maybe other folks would laugh all the harder. That made me mad.

That night Sophia and I lay in our beds next to each other in our room. When Soph was restless, I sat on the end of her cot and petted her fine wavy hair.

It felt like stroking the cat. Tonight we were both restless.

"Abby, are you scared about going to Boston?"

"Some, I guess." I kept petting her hair. The mixed feelings turned over inside me. "But I want to go. It'll be noisy but exciting. Like Andover on Independence Day."

"You won't let loose of my hand? I won't get lost?"

"Soph, don't be scared of that. Finish your prayers and go to sleep."

I didn't tell Sophia about my *real* fears. Not of leaving home or getting lost, but fear that I would never learn all the lessons. Fear that I'd disgrace the doctor and not be a good enough leader. Fear that I'd find the magic road didn't lead anywhere for us.

Sophia was floating away to dream her dream. So I lay in bed and drifted off to join her.

3
Others Like Us

Twenty whole miles from home, Papa said. How many hours in our wagon? How many jolts, how many stops? How many funny smells? How many strange noises? A bigger number than Richard could put down on his slate?

"Papa, what are those birds crying? What are those men shouting? What's that cracking sound?"

"We're by the sea now. Those crying birds are gulls. Those men are hauling goods off great ships. The cracking sounds are the sails that make the ships move in the wind. Now let me hold the horse, girls."

We clung to the seat as we swerved left and right.

The sound of wheels on cobblestones exploded in our ears. Papa yelled and said a few oaths at the hackney drivers who were about to push us off the road.

Sophia started moaning in fear. I hung on to her and the seat at the same time. Soon the ships and gulls were gone, and we heard a swish-swish. The scent of fresh-cut hay filled my nose.

"Where are we now?" I asked Papa.

"By a great meadow. A sign calls it the Common."

"What's that swishing?"

"A row of boys cutting down the grass with sickles."

The sound of a horse galloping hard beside us made us jump. Papa called out, "By the devil himself! How can a man drive and read directions in this city!"

It amazed me to hear Papa swear. "Papa, you're looking for a neck of land, aren't you? With water on both sides?"

"Yes," Papa said. "Dr. Howe's is on Pleasant Street." The wagon rolled around a corner. "There's the sign," Papa said. He pulled our horse up by the roadside and tied him, then carried Sophia down in his arms. I knew she was clinging to him as she'd been clinging to me.

As I got myself down, I heard a door open. A familiar voice called to us. My heart jumped—I'd heard that voice for twelve weeks in my dreams.

"Mr. Carter, welcome! Abigail, Sophia! Come into the house and meet the other pupils." Doctor Howe's voice was full of smiles.

Papa led Sophia and me down a path of bricks. The doctor took us into his large front parlor, where folks were waiting. I smelled cakes and ginger punch and the scents of city people, which were sweet and spicy as flowers. If only I could rush around the room and feel everything. But now wasn't the time. I had to behave properly.

"Ladies and gentlemen," Doctor Howe said, "this is Abigail and Sophia Carter. And their father, Mr. Carter. They are from Andover. I'm seating them on chairs before the hearth. I'd like each of you to come shake their hands."

Folks greeted us like we did Pastor after church. I tried to get an idea of each pupil from the size and feel of their hands as Doctor placed each hand in mine.

"This is Maria Penniman," Doctor said. "Her family lives in Cambridge, by Harvard College. Maria is eighteen."

Maria had a slim little hand, smooth and delicate. I knew she didn't do chores. When she said hello, she sounded like a shy but sweet girl.

"And this is Charles Morrill, from Wilmington, north of Boston. You passed his town on your way from Andover."

Charles was almost twenty, with a rich speaking voice and a fine-boned hand.

"This is Benjamin Bowen," Doctor continued. "He's thirteen and helps in his father's carpentry shop in Marblehead. His home is on the ocean, near Salem."

I liked Ben from his hand, already firm and rough like a workingman's. But his boy's voice still cracked sometimes.

"And last is Joseph Smith, come all the way from Portsmouth, New Hampshire. He is ten like you, Abby. We'll call him Young Joe so as not to confuse him with my own brother Joseph Howe."

"Joe," I said, "did you come all that way in a wagon?"

Joe shook my hand fast, then jumped back. "I came with my father on a clipper," he said proudly. "It sailed so fast and the wind blew so loud, it was grand."

A real ship! I liked Joe already. He was a traveler who was fond of adventure.

Doctor brought over his sisters. "This is Miss Elizabeth and Miss Jeanette. They are my younger sisters and will teach you handiwork." Elizabeth seemed tall like the doctor, but Jeanette was smaller and had tiny hands. They welcomed us and put plates of cakes in our laps. Doctor Howe told us his father, Mr. Howe, and his brother Mr. Joseph were across the parlor.

Someone mentioned his stepmother, Mrs. Howe, who did not talk with us. Then we met his widowed sister, Mrs. Babcock, who lived in her own house but would come each day to teach music. A lady called Cook Sarah, who kept the house, greeted us in her funny way of speaking. She talked Irish, I learned later. She smelled delicious like the oven on baking day.

After a while my head spun with new voices. Sophia whispered, "I forgot all their names. Except for Cook Sarah."

"Never mind," I said. "We'll keep asking."

Finally Papa said he'd better take the horse to the stable to feed and get himself a room for the night. Time had come to say good-bye. We went to the front door with him.

Papa kissed our cheeks and squeezed our hands.

"Papa, I'm scared I'll miss you too much," Sophia said, sniffling.

"Be brave like Abby," he said. "Do your lessons good. Me and Mam and the boys will pray for you every day."

"We have our teachers and four new blind friends." I smiled at Papa. I still could hardly believe it was true. "I'll look after Soph."

"That's my Abby. When the baby comes, I'll put it down in a letter. The doctor can read it to you."

"Papa, maybe someday we can write our words and put them in the post to you!" Such an amazing notion made me giggle.

"That will be the proudest day of my life," Papa said with a husky voice. Then he bent to my ear. "Listen, Abby. If this school gets too hard for Sophia, have the doctor send for me. I'll fetch her home."

"I will. Good-bye, Papa."

"Good-bye, my girls."

The front door closed, and Papa was gone. Sophia started to sob and squeeze my hand. Just then Miss Jeanette came to us.

"I'm to show you to your new room. It's on the third floor next to Maria's and beside Cook Sarah's. Will you come?"

Sophia reached out for Miss Jeanette. She liked her quiet, gentle way. As we went up the big stairs, Sophia gulped her tears and said, "You smell good. Like honeysuckle."

"That's my cologne," she said.

"If you dab some on each day," I said, "we'll know when you are with us from the scent."

"Then I shall. I have much to learn about you."

She didn't know we tried to recognize people by their scent and the sound of their paces, even before they spoke. Miss Jeanette and her family had never known blind people. They felt strange with us. Even

Doctor Howe did not know much more. I figured we would all have to learn together.

❧   ❧   ❧

Sophia and I shared a bed in a small room at the back of the house. Just when I thought Sophia had fallen asleep, she started whimpering again. "Hush now," I told her. "We have to sleep so we can start lessons tomorrow."

But Soph kept on crying.

A knock sounded at our door. "It's Maria," the voice said softly. "Is Sophia all right?"

"Come in," I said. "She's just missing home."

"Poor girl." Maria reached out and touched my shoulder. She sat beside Sophia. "She's just six, isn't she?"

"Almost seven," I said. Sophia stopped crying.

"That's very young to be away from home. And you and Young Joe are only ten?"

"Yes." I smoothed Sophia's sweaty hair.

"That's young too. But we are all the same age when it comes to lessons," Maria said. "Charles and I want to learn reading and writing the same as you do. Neither of us has ever been away from home."

Sophia sat up, curious to hear our conversation. "Are you missing home too?" she asked Maria.

"A little. It was safe at home. People read to me

and took care of me. Now I'm almost a woman. I want to read and look after myself as best I can."

"Why do we need to read?" Sophia asked.

"It's important," I said. "That way we can read the Scriptures for ourselves. And we can find out what's in somebody's head who lives far away."

"Abby's right," Maria said. "We can't just listen and try to store everything in our memory, like a big barn. We'll forget too much. In books you can call things back."

I told Maria, "You'll be the first to learn."

"I hope so," Maria said. "And I will love to learn writing. I hope to write letters and stories."

"We have three brothers at home," I told Maria. "The two older ones can see, but not always so good. Little Edward is blind. I want to send letters home to them."

"My brother Arthur is blind too," Maria said. "He's very smart."

"I've heard blindness sometimes comes in families," I said.

"Yes," Maria said. "But nobody knows why."

Sophia had fallen asleep. "We better sleep too," I whispered to Maria. "We meet our schoolmasters tomorrow."

Maria gave me a little hug. "Be brave, Abby. We must all help each other. Good night."

After Maria left our room, I lay down and closed

my eyes. "Dear Lord, please don't let the loneliness for home make me cry too," I asked. But the loneliness did hit me, like a wave of pain. We were so far from the night sounds of the farm. I would not be with Mam and Papa and the boys for a long time. I pressed my face in the pillow and cried a few tears. Then I screwed up my courage. If I could learn at this school, I swore I'd be the strong one.

🌙 4
Spying

I woke up from a deep sleep to strange bedroom smells. I reached over and felt Sophia beside me in bed. Where were we? Oh yes, the small room up three sets of steps in Doctor Howe's home. We were at school!

Sophia slept soundly. The night vapors had filled our room. Cool damp clung to our sheets. How could I tell the time without the livestock to call me? I felt for the door, then stuck out my head. No sounds came from the hallway.

Was it still night? I went back to our open window and leaned out. Although the Howes did not keep chickens or cows, someone in Boston must keep

them. I listened but heard no crowing or lowing. Did
Boston roosters sleep late?

Then I heard slow creaky steps on the floor below.
Was it Cook Sarah, heading for the kitchen? I put on
fresh pantalets, stockings, and a smock from my travel
box. I brushed and plaited my hair. No one came to
fetch us. And I had to use the privy. We were all given
chamber pots for our privy doings. But I didn't like
pots. I remembered that the night before we had been
taken to a privy behind the house, down a path of fine
stones. I figured I could feel my way out there, then
get back to our room before Sophia even missed me.

As I worked my way down the stair, I heard someone stumbling on the landing below me. Ben or
Young Joe? Then a deep voice spoke an oath. It was
the doctor, stumbling on his own stair. I crept behind
him, tiptoeing. Doctor was bumping into things. Why
didn't he turn and talk to me? Then he headed for the
kitchen. I followed toward the sound of Cook Sarah
banging coals onto the stove grate. She said loudly,
"Lord have mercy, Doctor. You gave me a start, rising
so early. Are your eyes ailing you, sir?"

"No, Sarah. It's just a blindfold. Ouch. What did I
knock into?"

"The butcher block, sir."

"I thought surely I'd remember where that thing was.
I'll be unlocking the back door now and going out."

"Yes, Doctor. I'll get the key for you."

"No, I must find it myself. Damnation!"

"You wrapped your shin on the coal scuttle."

"Sarah, please, go set up the dining room. Now where's that key ring? Ow!"

"As you say, sir. I'll be leaving now."

This was the funniest conversation I ever heard. The doctor had bound his eyes? I tried not to giggle. I heard Cook Sarah pass through the pantry into the dining room. So I moved back down the hall to better hear the doctor.

First he grumbled. Then he dropped the key ring. I heard it clatter across the floor. Then he struggled to get the right key in the keyhole. The whole time he made oaths and cries. At last he got out the door. By this time, we both wanted to get to that privy in a terrible way.

It took the doctor forever to get down the path. He was trying to be like us, but he was doing a poor job of it. As I followed him, unknown, I knew I was being a spy.

How could Doctor be lost in his own garden? He didn't use his toes or hands or ears, or even his nose. As the breeze came off the river, it told me where that privy was. Finally I heard the privy door open and shut. So I stood behind a bush and waited. Would he keep his eyes blinded all day? How long

before he could not stand to live the way I lived my whole life?

After the doctor came out, tripping and mumbling, I knew he had not given up the game yet. So I slipped into the privy, still playing the spy.

❧   ❧   ❧

For breakfast I was put by Sophia between Miss Jeanette and Miss Elizabeth. Across the big dining room table, Young Joe and Benjamin sat between Doctor and Mr. Joseph. Maria and Charles were seated at the ends. Maybe those were the chairs used by old Mr. and Mrs. Howe? Since the Howes were not farmers, they just stayed abed as late as they pleased. No one said to wait for them.

"Let us all say where we are seated," Doctor said. "And let us feel who is beside us."

He didn't say a word about wearing his blindfold. I was the only one in on his secret. Except his family could see, couldn't they? They must have thought he'd gone feebleminded!

We listened and drew pictures in our heads about where things were set on a strange table. No one wanted to bump elbows with the grown-ups. Cook Sarah set Scotch oatmeal with molasses and cream before us. It tasted so fine, I forgot about being the spy and kept spooning it in. Soon Cook Sarah passed a fragrant platter under our noses.

"I've got a heap of muffins and jam here," she said. Then she stopped. "Doctor, what am I to do? Put their hands to the platter?"

"We shall ask. Abby?"

"Yes, Doctor."

"What happens at your table at home? Does your mother have you touch the platters? Or does she fill your plate?"

I smiled at Doctor asking *me* how to act at table. Then I remembered. He was trying to learn about we blind. And he could not see the platter himself.

"We tell Mam what we want. And she puts it on our plate," I told him.

"And your cup?"

"She puts it in our hands so we set it and know the place."

"Very well. Sarah, that is what we shall do here."

"Yes, Doctor."

Doctor's brother Mr. Joseph spoke up in a gruff way. "Sarah, I have to get to the factory. May I help myself?"

"Yes, sir, I'm coming. Lord have mercy, so many new rules."

Finally we got cups of cider put in our hands. I whispered to Sophia, "Set your cup right. If we spill, Mr. Joseph will shout us good."

Then Doctor asked, "Do you all have plenty to eat?"

We all said we surely did.

"Ask Cook Sarah for anything you want. Today we are going to learn where everything is in the house. Your teachers, Mr. Trencheri and Mr. Pringle, will come over from their boardinghouse to meet you. For now, just eat while your food is . . . drat."

Young Joe said, "Somebody spilled my cider, but it wasn't me."

All we pupils giggled, except Benjamin. He felt around and said, "I didn't do it, Joe. Don't blame me."

Mr. Joseph said, "I believe it was the doctor, young man. He is playing some kind of ridiculous game."

I smiled, for I knew all along. Miss Elizabeth tapped her fingers on the table and said, "Oh, dear," to herself. She was a nervous sort of spinster lady.

"It is not a game, Joseph," said Doctor.

"It is upsetting enough around here," Mr. Joseph said. He shoved back his chair. "I'm going to the factory before you dump your cup on me!"

We all stayed quiet while he stomped out of the room. When I felt Sophia's hand steal into my lap for comfort, I gave it a squeeze.

Then the doctor spoke. "I'm sorry, Joe. I tipped your cider. I have jam stuck to my hand. And I can't find my napkin."

Young Joe sat in silence.

"What do you think is wrong with me?" Doctor asked.

"I know," I said.

"Who said that?"

"Me, Abby."

"Yes, Abby?"

"What's wrong is you've bound your eyes. So you can be blind like us."

"You have guessed correctly. But not for a silly game. I must get through this first day by understanding what you endure. I must try not to get hurt or lost or forget a single thing. I must never lose my temper. I must, for one day, be like you."

Although we all thought the same thing, only Benjamin had the spunk to say it. "Doctor . . . if you want to be like us, somebody has to make fun of you or trick you. Or pay you no mind, like you were a dog."

Doctor cleared his throat. "So, Ben. You think I must be tricked or teased."

"Yes," said Benjamin.

"I'm afraid he is right," Charles added.

I knew I had to confess. What I did was wrong. "Doctor, you have been tricked. By me."

"Abby? How is that?"

"I knew you bound your eyes. I heard you stumble and tell Cook Sarah. I heard you say oaths making your way to the privy. I followed you."

Everyone sucked in his breath, waiting for Doctor to let me have a tongue-lashing. But he kept his voice steady.

"Then you were spying on me?" he said.

"I guess I was," I said, embarrassed. "But being blind, I just listened in. Like always."

"I thank you for my lesson in being blind. I do *not* like being tricked."

"Doctor," said Ben, "will you keep blindfolded all day?"

"Yes," said Doctor. "Even if I end up crawling on my hands and knees. I may get rather mean by then. But I must do it."

We all admired Doctor. He was brave to try so hard. But soon he would see in a way that we would not. And that made us different forever.

Then Sophia spoke up. "Doctor, we have to do one other thing at our table."

Doctor said, "Sophia? Please tell me all."

"When we spill, we have to mop it up. And you spilled Joe's cider."

"Young miss!" Sarah said. "You can't speak so!"

"Please, Sarah," said Doctor. "Today Sophia is my teacher. Just bring me a towel."

I grinned and slowly shook my head. We had surely landed at an amazing school.

❧ 5
Blindman's Buff

When we finished breakfast and Mr. Joseph had gone to work, a knock sounded on the front door. The doctor scooted back his chair, rattling his cup and spoon. "That will be your teachers, Trencheri and Pringle. I'll go to the door." Then he paused. "Stay quiet," he said to us still at table, with a devilish tone in his voice. "No one tells them I have bound my eyes. Let's see if I can trick them."

We grinned to hear the doctor do some mischief. The blindfolding made Miss Elizabeth jumpy. Whispering, "Oh, dear," she began to clear the table. Miss Jeanette stayed stiff in her seat. I said to Sophia, "Those teachers will know something is funny. Otherwise they aren't smart enough to be teachers."

Sophia was tired of sitting at table. She asked, "Miss Jeanette, can we go in the front parlor? We can wait for the teachers there." She also wanted to listen in. So did I!

"I suppose so," Miss Jeanette said. "Follow me."

We all trailed after the swish of her long skirts. She gathered us by the hearth. We overheard Doctor bid good morning to our teachers from the foyer.

"We've finished breakfast," he said. "Come in the dining room and meet your pupils."

I expect Miss Jeanette did not know what to do, for we heard her sighing. Then we heard the teachers follow Doctor down the center hall to the dining room, tapping canes as they walked.

"Doctor," Mr. Trencheri said, "are you not well? You seem a bit unsteady."

"I'm fine," Doctor said. "Never better. Here we are in the dining room. By the buffet. Pupils, here are your teachers."

Sophia and Joe were stifling giggles. Miss Jeanette stood stone still. Then Mr. Trencheri, who came from the place called France, said, "I believe there are no other persons here, Doctor. Is this some sort of test?"

Mr. Pringle, from Scotland, added, "Sure, Doctor, you don't mean to insult us?"

"Insult you? No! I only meant to say, the students were here . . . but not now. And it is I who am taking the test, Trencheri. For this day, and believe me, it will be the longest day of my life, I wear the blindfold."

"Ah!" said Mr. Trencheri. "You bind your eyes? To gain sympathy with the children?"

"Yes."

Mr. Pringle laughed. "So you're playing blindman's buff, is it?"

Doctor also gave a chuckle. "Pringle, let's see if we can win *this* game and find the students."

We heard the men start toward the dining room door. Miss Jeanette whispered, "We'd best go into the foyer. We don't want Mr. Trencheri to get angry at *us*."

We followed her into the foyer just as Doctor and the teachers came down the hall. Old Mr. Howe and his wife marched down the staircase. And we all collided.

"What's this running about?" old Mr. Howe said. "Samuel, it is past nine—"

"Mr. Howe," his wife interrupted. "What ails your son? He has a bandage on his eyes!"

"Oh, Samuel," Miss Jeanette said, "the pupils wanted to go into the parlor. . . ."

Old Mr. Howe boomed, "We can't have such a commotion!"

The doctor spoke up like a real schoolmaster. "I am sorry, Father. You and Mother please go to the dining room for your breakfast. Gentlemen, you remember my family who you met last week. Let's get this school day started. Everyone, follow me!"

The doctor turned around and walked thump-bang into the front door. We pupils tried not to laugh. Mr. Trencheri spoke up. "Doctor, I know you are our director. But I will not follow you into closed doors. It sets a bad example for the children. They must learn to use the outstretched hand, the slippered foot, and the walking stick."

We sensed that Mr. Trencheri was short, whereas the doctor was tall and proud like a soldier. And we could tell that Mr. Trencheri was young from his voice, whereas Doctor was older. But if we followed Mr. Trencheri, he would teach us how to get around the whole world.

"Mr. Trencheri," the doctor said, "and Mr. Pringle. Please lead on. We shall follow."

All day we roamed around the Howes' house. We practiced using the outstretched hand and the slippered foot. Benjamin and Charles took lessons with Mr. Trencheri's walking stick. They tapped it from side to side in a space as wide as their body. That way they checked for a clear path. We made pictures in our heads of where the doors and stairs and chairs would be found.

After luncheon, we gathered in front of the parlor

hearth. Doctor said to us, "I like a good contest! Let's see who is the fastest one to find things."

Mr. Pringle said, "Sounds like blindman's buff again."

Doctor replied, "Pupils, who is the first to find Cook Sarah without bumping into anything? And prime the pump? Who is the fastest to touch the end of our property's fence? On your mark . . . and go!"

It wasn't much of a contest. Young Joe and I always won. Sophia would get turned around and lose track of me and sit down and whine, "Abbeeee." And Maria, who was such a soft heart, would stop playing the game and comfort her. I was first to find Sarah, first to the privy, and first to pump a bucket of water from the kitchen cistern. Ben and Charles weren't daring, but Joe was amazingly fast. He found his way all around the fence before most of us got a start.

Doctor kept stumbling and banging, going "oof" and "ouch," ripping his trousers. By day's end, he was still "blind."

That evening before supper we went up to our rooms to wash in our basins and comb our hair. I heard a horse get put in the stable and the door open and slam shut. I knew it must be grumpy Mr. Joseph, the doctor's brother, home from his glass factory. I decided to creep down the stairwell and listen.

". . . with this madness throughout the house. You

will send yourself to the hospital or the rest of us to the lunatic asylum. You must give this up!"

"No, Joseph," Doctor replied. "Providence sent me these pupils. I am learning how they learn and what they endure. In six months, they will show you. . . ."

"Six months? The family won't last that long."

"They must."

"I can't talk to you when you wear that fool blindfold."

"But I can *hear* you. And probably so can Miss Abby, whose ears are sharper than a fox's."

I wondered if Mr. Joseph looked up the stairwell and caught me spying. Or did he not bother? Like most folks, he hated talking to blind people because he could not know if they understood. My brother Justin explained it to me like this: "It's like talking to somebody who's in another room. You can't be sure what they hear or think. Eyes are like windows. Folks are used to looking inside them."

"Samuel, time is past for you to dash around the world like a knight," said Mr. Joseph. "You are always fighting wars and saving the poor. Now you are over thirty. Must I support this family without some help? Father's investments are dwindling."

"I know you are the dependable one," Doctor admitted. "Try to share my faith. In six months these pupils will be able to learn the same things that seeing children do. They will lead all the blind in New England. I beg you, Joseph."

Mr. Joseph sighed. "I haven't refused you yet," he said, "but this time Father may."

I heard heavy footsteps on the stair, so I darted back up to my room. Sophia was waiting with Maria.

"Abby? Where have you been?" Sophia said. "Spying?"

"Doctor and Mr. Joseph were arguing."

"Just like our brothers do?" Sophia asked.

"Mr. Joseph called him a knight and said he should stop fighting wars. Maria, what did he mean?"

"A knight?" Maria asked. "I'm not sure. I think in the old days, it was a man who saved people who needed help. I don't know who it was that Doctor saved. Or in what war."

"I guess it doesn't matter," I mumbled.

But I wondered if it was *us* that he wanted to save. And if the war was going on right in his own house.

"Maria, guess what else Doctor told Mr. Joseph? He said we can learn all the same things as seeing children learn. In only six months!"

"Oh, my!" said Maria. "That is so little time."

"We can't do it," said Sophia. "Can we?"

I thought about Richard and Justin and how they could read and write and put numbers on their slate. It took them more than *six years* to learn all that, because Justin started school the year Sophia was born.

I said, "We can learn a lot. I'm sure of it! We have to pretend it's a contest."

"Oh, Abby," Maria said sadly, "if only the contest were blindman's buff. That's the only one we can play."

Of course I never joined in running games and contests with the girls at Andover picnics. They didn't ask me, knowing I could never win at tag or run-right-through. But learning was like a game. I could win by reading just as well and as fast as other girls, couldn't I? This idea made me more determined than ever to prove Doctor was right. We *could* learn the same as anyone else.

❧ 6

Hard Lessons

Lessons came each day, one upon another. Numbers and writing in the dining room! Reading and recitation in the parlor! Handicrafts in the carriage house and cellar! Music at the pianoforte! Walking skills in the garden! School was everywhere.

Those letters and numbers had so many ways they could go together. Learning them could make your head hurt like a hammer knocking between your eyes. First the teachers gave us blocks to hold and touch. On each block was a carved letter or a number. Mr. Trencheri helped us run our pointer finger up and down and around them. When we felt the letters and the numbers, we said their names out loud, like a song.

We sang their sounds out loud too, like *kuh* for the letter *c*, *tuh* for the letter *t*, and so on. *Kuh* and *tuh*, *puh* and *duh*; we sounded like we were spitting out a mouthful of feathers. As for learning what to do with numbers, Sophia and I already knew how to count things. We'd counted up the eggs from the hens and such for Mam. Ben had counted boards in his father's shop. And Maria had counted stitches, being a fine knitter. But Charles and Young Joe were dreadful with numbers if they went higher than their ten fingers. They never needed to know before. Doctor didn't tease them about it. He just made them practice on the numbers all the more.

I told Doctor, "My older brothers put their numbers on a slate, to hold while they work with them. Richard said blind pupils would need a magic slate. Do you have one?"

Doctor said, "Blind pupils must learn in a different way than your brothers do. Mr. Trencheri has a case to hold your number blocks. He has another to make your letter blocks stand in line. These cases will work best for you."

I smiled as I thought about telling my brother, "Richard, we *do* have magic slates."

After our numbers lesson one day, Sophia told me it was funny that she knew more numbers than Charles did, since she just turned seven and he was twenty.

"Remember what Maria said," I reminded her. "We are all your age when it comes to lessons."

The truth was we were *not* all the same. Sophia was still little. The lessons wearied her head. She got aches and sniffles and sometimes dozed off during our afternoon work. At night she got weepy from missing Mam and Papa and the boys and the farm. I was pulling her to get her through the day. That wearied me too.

After three weeks, Mr. Trencheri started putting the letters together in a case to make up words. Like *kuh* and *aah* and *tuh*. Trace it with your fingers, speak it out your mouth, and *cat* was born. Letters and numbers were always dancing in my mind. That letter *p* was the best—tall like a fence post, with a round part tacked on like a cup handle and a sound like popcorn, *puh-puh!* I couldn't stop thinking of words that started with *p*, even when I was so tired I started bumping into things.

Soon we lined up the numbers into sums. Like ten and five put together is one-five, fifteen! Sums and words were like objects in your drawers: you set in your mind where they were and pulled them out each time you needed them.

Sophia was always a little behind us. Her mind was like her legs—short and sweet. It could not race along.

One afternoon we were having our recess. Doctor let us sweep together the leaves that had fallen into a great heap, then play in the pile. As I leaped with Ben and Joe, I heard Doctor call for Sophia. After a while he came back and took me aside.

"Abby," he said, "while she was waiting to play, Sophia lay down under the big oak. She fell asleep with her hands full of acorns. Do you think our school is too much for her?"

"No," I said. "Just too fast."

"I see," said Doctor. "We have been hurrying our lessons. But Sophia must stay well. That is the most important thing."

"Yes, Doctor."

I knew that if Sophia got too sad or sickly, Papa would come and fetch her home. Even though we were scrappy and she wore me out, I did not want her to leave me. She was my only sister.

"Stroll around the garden with Maria," Doctor told me. "I will watch Sophia while she naps."

I wanted to leap some more in the leaves with Joe and Ben. But I did as Doctor said. Maria was lady-like. Since I was over ten, I was trying to behave more like her.

"Maria?" I called out. "Where are you?"

"Down the path beyond the vegetable garden," she called back.

I practiced the outstretched hand and the slippered foot. The street sounds and the breeze from the river stayed on my left. That way I found the path to the garden. Maria waited for me until we touched hands.

"You're doing very well with your strolling," Maria said as we walked along the fence. "I imagine you can find your way all over your farm at home."

"Yes. Hope I don't forget how."

"I always have walked with a guide," Maria said. "Strolling alone is hard. I hate to think I will fall and look foolish."

"Who cares?" I said. "Seeing children fall down too. Maybe your smock gets a little dirty. . . ."

"*Ladies* don't fall down," Maria corrected me.

"Oh. I guess you're right."

Soon we were strolling along the part of the fence on busy Pleasant Street. Folks drove their carriages and walked the path that ran beside the Howes' property. Sometimes they stopped and watched us while we played at recess. We could hear little children's high voices as they giggled and called us funny names. The older ladies' voices would go "ahh" and call us poor pathetic things. One gentleman wondered out loud how young Doctor Howe got himself into such a peculiar business. Although no one bothered us, strangers made Maria nervous.

As we strolled, some young ladies stopped to talk and watch. I figured from their voices they were about Maria's age. But they were giggling like ignorant babies. One of them said, "Look how they stick out their hands and feet. They strut like toy soldiers!"

Since Doctor told us *never* to answer back to strangers, I kept on strolling. But Maria stopped. She gasped like someone had smacked her. I couldn't tell what she was doing. But she must have gotten confused and tripped. I heard a thump and a yelp. The young ladies burst out giggling.

I stooped and felt around. "Did you fall, Maria?" I asked. "I'll help you up."

Although I reached Maria's shoulder, she did not rise. She knelt on the grass and started to weep. At that minute, Ben came over. He had ears almost as keen as mine, and he heard Maria fall and cry.

"What's this?" Ben asked. "Is Maria all right?"

"Some young ladies were making fun of her and she fell," I whispered over Maria's weeping.

"Hey, you ladies!" Ben yelled loud as he could. "Get away from this property! You got no right to make fun of us. Maria is twice as smart and pretty as you are. You stupid cows!" He gave the fence a furious kick.

There was a minute of weird silence. The young ladies quit laughing. Maria quit weeping. Even the carriage traffic stopped. The minute seemed like

forever. Then we heard the sound of someone striding hard and fast across the grass.

"Benjamin Bowen!" Doctor's deep voice rang out. "Did you answer back to these young ladies?"

"Yes . . . but . . ."

"Benjamin, you will apologize."

"I . . . apologize."

"Maria, if you are not hurt, then get to your feet."

Maria took my hand and stood up in silence. I thought I could hear her heart pounding.

"The three of you will wait on the back porch for me. Recess is *over*."

As we walked to the porch, Maria whispered in a bitter tone, "They called us toy soldiers. So awkward and ugly. And when I fell, they laughed. It is so hard for a lady to be blind."

"But Maria," I said, "Ben took up for you."

"Yes," Maria said. "And I thank him. But we have been told never to answer back. Now Doctor must punish him."

"I'm glad I did it," Ben said. "I been switched before. A boy like me can take it."

I knew Ben meant having his hands or backside whipped with a switch. My brothers got switched at school. Because they didn't see too well, their schoolmaster thought they were dull or lazy. Sometimes Papa even switched them for quarreling instead of working.

"I don't think it's fair," I told Ben. "You were taking up for Maria. Boys have to do that for girls, don't they?"

Ben didn't answer. We sat on the porch, listening and waiting. Charles and Young Joe joined us. Miss Jeanette came out to ring her bell that meant recess was over.

"You're already here," she said. "Where is Sophia?"

"Napping under the big oak," I said.

"Oh, dear. I will get her." And she walked off to fetch Sophia, who slept through all the trouble.

Finally Doctor returned. He called to Mr. Trencheri and Mr. Pringle to come outside. They were taking their tea in the kitchen during our recess.

"Trencheri, Pringle, Ben has been rude to a group of young ladies at our gate. He must be punished."

Everyone remained quiet.

"How were the boys punished in France?" Doctor asked.

Mr. Trencheri said, "With the switch, Doctor."

"And in Scotland?"

"The same, Doctor," said Mr. Pringle.

"When I was a boy, I went to Boston Latin School. I got punished many times. Mostly for fighting with other boys, who were cruel to the younger ones. My hands got beaten to jelly. Being switched did not make me wiser or more humble. I vowed I would not switch my children."

We were all fair amazed to hear Doctor tell us this secret about his youth.

"While I am the director of this school," Doctor said, "no pupils will be beaten with the switch or the rod. For one week, Benjamin will do all the boys' chores. He will haul all the wood in the morning. He will take out all the trash to the compost heap and the ashpit. He will do all this extra work during recess instead of playing. And he will remember never to be rude again."

Maria squeezed my hand, glad that Ben would not get switched for standing up for her. But I scowled, steaming like a pot that won't boil. As we went back into the house for our classes, Ben whispered, "A whole week's chores. Better to get switched and get it over!"

None of us said a word. I guess Doctor saw the expression on my face. As the others went on, he stopped me.

"Abby, why are you looking so angry?"

I decided I'd speak out, even if I got the same punishment. "Those ladies were cruel to laugh at Maria. They made her fall. Ben stood up for her. He was right!"

"Those young ladies were cruel because they don't understand blind people. Many more like them will come to see our school. We have to keep giving them a chance to learn. Until no one is ignorant anymore."

I never looked at it like that before.

"Ben only thought about today," Doctor said. "I must think about all our tomorrows. Now get to your lessons."

Back in class, I was well into lining up my numbers when I realized that *I* had talked back to Doctor. And he never punished me at all.

❧ 7

A Black Swan

One morning we pupils and teachers gathered around the dining room table for our lesson in reading words. Doctor said, "Mr. Trencheri thinks you are ready to start reading from a book. So here they are. The only two raised-print books in English I could find in the world."

We'd been so occupied with spelling and writing words with our letter cases that we never even thought about books. Yet here they were: magic books for people who could not see the pages. As I touched these huge treasures, a thrill went through my finger-tips to my heart. The raised letters on the covers spelled the names of the books: *English Stories* and the

Gospel of Saint John, from the Bible. As I traced them, I could barely make them out.

"They come from Pringle's school," Mr. Trencheri said. "My school in France has many books for the blind. But they are in the French language." He raised the cover of the *Stories* and put my finger on the first page.

"Oh, the letters are so *small*," I said. "I can't tell what they are."

"You will learn, Miss Abby," said Mr. Trencheri. "Soon your fingertips will fly down the page."

First a magic slate, and now magic books! Would my brothers ever believe it?

By the end of the week, we were tired from trying to read the first story in our book. Only Maria, with her delicate fingers used to needlework, could follow the letters. Joe and Ben mostly fumbled and mumbled. Charles pressed his finger this way and that but couldn't figure it out either. Sophia and I got some of the letters, missed others. We all got headaches from thinking so hard.

"One day it will all come to you," Mr. Trencheri said. "Like after you have been in a cold dark room and you go into the blazing sun and you have a . . . what is the word? A *flash* of light?"

"Mr. Trencheri, I have that flash sometimes," I said. "Do all blind people?"

Doctor perked up and came to me. "What flash is that, Abby?"

"Sometimes if I wake up from a nap, and I open my eyes with the hot sun right in my face, I see a flash. I want to reach up and touch the light. But it goes away."

Doctor put his hand on my shoulder. "The light Mr. Trencheri is talking about will never fade away. It will stay inside you."

"What kind of light is that, Doctor?" Sophia asked.

"The light you get from knowledge. Now, back to lessons."

As we went on trying to read, we heard a wagon being driven around into the Howes' yard. The driver banged on the back door. We knew Cook Sarah answered, because we could hear her fussing.

"Doctor Howe, if you please," said Sarah as she came to our doorway. "A cartman has put a great tin tub on our porch. He says you ordered it."

"Ah, our tub!" Doctor got excited. "Just in time for the weekend. We shall christen it tonight!"

"Doctor," Sarah said, "is it for washing the linen?"

"It is for washing *us*."

"Lord have mercy. Such a household."

Later that evening, Doctor hauled the tin tub into the kitchen. He pumped and poured. He heated kettle after kettle and poured them too. Soon the tub was full of warm water. Miss Jeanette and Miss Elizabeth joined us to watch.

"We will have modern bathing practices in this house," Doctor announced. "This is 1832, and we will bathe every week. It is good for the skin and circulation."

"Even in the winter when it's cold?" I asked.

"Absolutely, Abby. It isn't cold in this kitchen. You and Sophia and Maria will bathe first. Sarah will attend you. Then we will bail out the tub and fill it with fresh warm water for Charles, Joe, and Ben. Lastly, I will enjoy a fine brisk scrub myself."

Miss Jeanette and Miss Elizabeth must have been so shocked, they could hardly talk. Young ladies were supposed to sponge themselves from basins in their chambers! Finally Miss Jeanette said, "We have handi-work to do." And they hustled out of the kitchen.

"Charles," Doctor said, "please take the boys into the parlor for a singing lesson. I'll call when it is your turn."

The boys hurried out right fast also. They didn't trust this idea of scrubbing your whole body every week. Doctor told Sarah, "Please go fetch a stack of towels, a bar of mild soap, and the girls' nightdresses."

She marched off to do it, while muttering about catching our death and shameful doings and such. While she was gone, Doctor explained to us why going naked into a tub of water was good. But when he talked like a real doctor, we did not always understand.

Soon Sarah returned, along with old Mrs. Howe. She smelled like stale spice and had a shrill crackly voice. "What in the name of heaven is this?" she said to Doctor.

"A bathing tub, ma'am."

"Young ladies without clothes in my kitchen? It is shocking."

"We don't mind, Mrs. Howe," I said. "We can't see each other anyway."

Mrs. Howe couldn't think what to say to that. She just sputtered. Then she said to me, "Young lady, when your father hears of this, I am sure he will insist you go home!" And she stomped off. Doctor said, "Girls, scrub briskly. Rinse well. Towel off completely. Sarah, call me when they are in their nightclothes. I will be in the parlor with the boys. And don't worry about your parents. They will trust me. Bathing is the wave of the future!"

And into that tub we went, splashing and scrubbing, and wondering what wild notion Doctor would have next.

The following Sunday after church service, Sophia and I were walking down the path to the privy. We heard old Mrs. Howe talking to Mr. Howe in the

garden. She said in her shrill crackly way, ". . . I know you will do what your children want, sir. You always do. But I must have my say."

"Fair enough, ma'am," said Mr. Howe. Then I guess he saw us girls. "Please to keep your voice down some," he told her. "They are blind, not deaf."

"Why bother, when them children is everywhere! The neighbors shy from us like we have the plague. Now I hear from Joseph that they may be here through the holidays?"

"I have given Samuel leave to try this idea," Mr. Howe said. "It is his dream."

"You have given Samuel *leave* all of his life. Bringing home a half-dozen poor blind! Why you put up with him, I do not understand."

Sophia and I figured that the Samuel she meant was Doctor. His own stepmother did not like him much.

Mr. Howe replied loudly but firmly, "Ma'am, you must *try* to understand. Samuel's pranks won him whippings as a boy. Still, his late mother always told me: 'Samuel will ask much of you. But you must give it, because he is our black swan.' "

Mrs. Howe only went "Humph." Maybe, like me, she didn't know what a black swan was. But she talked no more of putting us out, just about making relish of the last of the green tomatoes.

After Sunday dinner, Sophia and I were in the kitchen with Maria, drying the flatware for Cook

Sarah. I decided I would ask them if they knew what a swan was.

Cook Sarah said, "Why, didn't they have no swans up at Andover? They're great lovely birds, larger than geese, with long curvy necks. They live on ponds and are white as snow."

"But how do you mean, white as snow?" I asked her.

"Poor blind child, how can I tell you? Why, snow and clouds and cream and such, 'tis white. White is pure, like no color at all." When Sarah went off to the dining room, I asked Maria, "Do you understand what she means?"

Maria replied, "Swans live on the pond on the Common. My family and I have gone for strolls there. I expect they are the fairest and strongest of all birds."

"But Maria, then what would a 'black swan' be?"

Maria said softly to us, "Black? I remember about black. I did not go blind until I caught the scarlet fever when I was three. Black is deep and dark and mysterious. It is all colors swirled into one. Black is everything."

"But if someone called you a black swan, would that be *good*?"

Maria said, "Where did you hear of a black swan?"

"Old Mr. Howe said that Doctor's dead mother used to call him that."

"What could she mean?" Sophia asked. "That he has a long neck? That he likes to swim in the pond?"

Maria decided, "A black swan would be different, all right."

That night after prayers, I thought more about it. Doctor had told us that we were different because we were blind. We learned in different ways. We got around the world in different ways. But we were still special. So I added, "Please let Doctor's parents think he is special enough to let him keep us in their house. At least until I finish learning to read those books."

❧ ❧ ❧

A few days later, I was the first one into the sitting room by the pianoforte for a music lesson. Mrs. Babcock, the doctor's widowed sister, played a piece. She called it an exercise. We were as fond of Mrs. Babcock as we were of Miss Jeanette. She taught us to sing and play the scales, up and down. I sat beside her.

"Mr. Trencheri says that in Paris, blind people play the piano and the organ. They even have a blind teacher for music at his old school. His name is Mr. Braille, and he is a great musician."

"So the doctor has told me," she said.

"Do you think that I could ever learn to play so well?" This was starting to be my secret dream. I hadn't told anyone about it.

"Do you mean well enough to play in public?"

"Yes, ma'am. Or would folks think it too peculiar?"

"Both you and Sophia show a talent for music. No, I don't think it's too peculiar. That is, if the doctor doesn't think so."

A talent. A talent! I liked that word and how it made me feel. I rolled it around on my tongue. A talent . . .

"Mrs. Babcock, do you know what a black swan is?"

"Now where did I ever hear that? Oh, my mother used to say it many years ago. I think it means rare. Unusual. You don't know what black is, do you?"

"No. Colors don't mean anything to me."

"Our mother used to call the doctor that. I think she meant that some people are special. They will try new ideas, travel new paths. Their ideas may seem a little odd to others. . . ."

"Like going naked into the big bathtub every week?"

Mrs. Babcock laughed softly. "I have heard tell of

that too. Yet the black swans are the ones that lead the rest of us. Maybe you are one of those people, Abby."

I had never wanted to be different. I wanted to be just like the other girls in Andover, the ones who could see and went to regular school and played at picnics. But now I thought that being a black swan might be the *best* way to be in the whole world.

❧ 8
Touching Home

One day at recess I noticed that leaves no longer fell from the oak trees. The Howes had uprooted their vegetable garden. The wind off the river had turned raw. When I felt such a chill on my face back on our farm, I knew winter was just beyond the northwest hills. How had Mam done without me this fall? Did our hay and corn harvest go well? Did our animals have enough feed for the winter? How many bags of beans had Mam dried? How many jars of fruit had she put up? Did she birth the baby? Did we have a new brother or sister? I kept quiet about it for fear of setting off Sophia's homesickness.

Doctor decided that we needed a map of our state,

Massachusetts. We would learn what he called geography and how to touch our hometowns. "If we had money to pay a printer, he could make us a raised map," said Doctor. "The boundaries of the state could be indented. All the rivers and towns could be raised. However, I shall have to make this map myself."

He described what he had in his hands, a heavy pasteboard and twine and glue. "With my pencil, I'm drawing the outlines of the states around us," he explained. "Our state is sandwiched between New York and the ocean. With Vermont and New Hampshire perched atop her head. And Connecticut and Rhode Island beneath her feet. She has hills on her west and a grand valley down the middle. We are in Boston, here on the northeastern edge."

"Will we be able to feel our towns?" I asked. "I can tell you, Andover's up the Essex Turnpike."

"What about me?" Young Joe said. "My town is in New Hampshire. Just atop your state's head."

"Be patient. All will be noted. Even Portsmouth."

Doctor gummed the twine everywhere he had drawn a border. His hands must have also got sticky, because he grumbled as he glued. My fingers were longing to skip back and forth between Boston and Andover on those roads.

"Touch it gently," Doctor warned. "Or that gummy twine will stick to you as it did to me."

"I don't follow how a map works," Joe said.

"This is hard to explain to you," said Doctor. "Suppose a seeing person is looking down. An anthill is at his feet. The ants are busy coming and going. They make trails all around the garden. The ants can't see anything but the ant in front of them. Yet the person can see all their trails. That is the view of the mapmaker."

"You mean a map tells us where all things are on the earth," said Ben.

"That's it, Ben. You now have the meaning of mapmaking."

"But Doctor," I said. "No one ever went high in the sky with the birds to look down. So how can we be sure our state is the shape that you marked it?"

"You are right to question, Abby. Mapmakers can make mistakes. Since I have traveled all around our state and the ones above and below, you can trust this map. Someday you may travel with me."

"Me?"

"That is my goal. To show people around the country what you have learned, so others will set. up schools for their blind."

Just then we heard a rapping at the front door.

"I will get it, Father," Doctor called. He left to answer it. We heard Doctor give a hearty greeting to a gentleman and some ladies in the foyer. Soon he returned to the dining room and brought along his visitors.

"Pupils," he said, "this is Mr. Horace Mann and his friends Misses Mary and Elizabeth Peabody. Mr. Mann is our head trustee. He is the best friend our school has."

"Hello, students," Mr. Mann said. And he went around the table and shook hands with each of us. He was tall and bony, but most kind and gentle.

We all said how d'you do.

"When *I* was a student at Brown College," said Doctor, "Mr. Mann was my language teacher."

"That I was," said Mr. Mann. "And now your Doctor Howe can speak Greek like a native."

Doctor laughed. "You know that is because I *lived* in Greece. But, Mann, you gave me a flying start."

Miss Elizabeth Peabody, the taller and bolder one, said, "Doctor Howe, I do so admire your book, *A Sketch of the Greek Revolution*. It is a great honor to meet you."

"Thank you, ma'am."

Doctor wrote a book? We didn't know this. I felt Mr. Mann lean over and touch our pasteboard. "What have we here?" he asked. "I believe one of you pupils has made a map?"

We all giggled. Doctor cleared his throat.

"In truth, Mann, *I* made it."

"Oh, Doctor," said Miss Elizabeth Peabody. "To think of the hero of the Greek war doing such humble work."

"It is because we lack money, ma'am. Or I should pay a proper mapmaker." Doctor paused. "I suppose you can't even tell what it is. . . ."

Mr. Mann spoke up. "I believe I see the boundary of our state. Abby, can you find Boston on it?"

"Yes, sir." I pointed it out.

"And what of your town?"

"Here, sir, it's Andover." I ran my finger up the Essex Turnpike, just as if I were traveling on it.

"And I hear you are learning to read, Abby?"

"Yes, sir. We learn from our letter blocks and now from our two books. I can read our first story."

"Splendid!" said Mr. Mann. "And you, Miss Maria, I hear your writing is coming along beautifully. And you, Benjamin, can do many sums on your number case. And you, Miss Sophia, have you learned your letters?"

"I have!" Soph said, and recited the whole alphabet so fast she made Mr. Mann laugh.

"And they are learning handicrafts with Mr. Pringle, and vocals and the piano with my sister Mrs. Babcock," said Doctor proudly. "Are they not wonderful?"

"They are," said Mr. Mann in a serious way. "In a few months they have passed what any seeing child could learn. But the rest of our trustees don't know this. Nor do our state legislators."

"The blind can learn as well as common school pupils," Doctor insisted.

"We must prove this," said Mr. Mann. "Do you believe that by January any of them will be reading with some skill?"

"*All* will be reading. Maria and Abby show skill now."

"Then here is my plan. In January, when the legislators gather at the statehouse, let us bring the pupils and their teachers. Let us bring their books and number cases and handicrafts. We will show the men with the power to help."

"What?" said Doctor. "You want my pupils to perform? As if they were on the stage?"

"No," said Mr. Mann. "This wouldn't be a show. Just a public examination."

Doctor sighed. "Call a meeting of the trustees at your office, Mann. And we will talk it over. I don't want to trouble the pupils with this idea now."

"Very well," said Mr. Mann. "Miss Mary, Miss Elizabeth, the evening grows late. We will call again."

"Yes, please do!" Doctor said, and he showed the folks to the door. While he walked off with them, I asked Maria, "What did Mr. Mann mean about legislators at the statehouse?"

"I don't know," said Maria. "The statehouse is in the city, across from the Common. It is where they make the laws."

Charles added, "And where they decide who gets money from the state treasury. That is what we must get. Money from the state to run our school."

"Oh!" I said. "That's it! We just need to go up and show those legislator fellows how we can do our lessons. And then they will give us the money."

Charles laughed. "Sounds simple enough."

"Not me, Abby," Sophia said. "I'd be taken with shyness before a bunch of strange fellows."

Ben said, "If you get your sums wrong, bet they laugh at you."

"Ben," said Charles, "you never get them wrong."

"Besides," I said, "our teachers won't let anyone fun us. And we'll do our lessons so well, nobody will have a chance."

Sophia leaned her head against me and yawned. "I

expect that day I'll just stay here with Cook Sarah and take a nap. And you get the money."

❧   ❧   ❧

Soon frost crunched on Boston's gardens. When a hard frost hit the farm, Papa brought in the last of the pumpkins and squash, and Mam made pies. I missed their sweet soft taste in my mouth. I missed Mam.

One day an extraordinary thing happened. Old Mr. Howe came home while we were having our noon recess. That was not unusual. He rode into town in his buggy most afternoons to read the newspapers, go to his bank, and get the mail at the post office. What was extraordinary was what he brought from the post office. Along with the letters for Doctor—who wrote to folks all around the world—this day he brought a letter for Sophia and me! It was the first mail we ever got.

Doctor took us into the parlor and sat us down. "This letter is from your father," he said. "I must read it to you."

Sophia and I wriggled with excitement.

Dear Daughters,

We pray each day that you are well. We wish to tell you that your new brother is here. He took a while coming. But he is a sweet fellow. Your mother calls him

Alonzo. Richard and Justin are working hard in school. Edward is a rascal without you girls to correct him. Your mother is still abed with the child, but doing well. The canning went good. We've put up ten bushels of dried apples and froze much cider. I butchered our hog for the winter. Haying went nicely before the rains. It is too soon to tell about the baby's eyes. Study well and do not disgrace the doctor. The Lord shall help you do his will. I'll come for you at Christmas.

> *Your loving Father,*
> *Richard Carter*

Sophia and I grabbed hands and squealed.

"Alonzo! What a fancy name! Oh, he's here!"

"I wish we could hold him right now!"

"Doctor," I said, "can we write some words to Mam and Papa and put them in the mail?"

"Yes indeed!" Doctor said. "I'll put paper in your writing board and help you spell the words."

We decided to write this: *We love Alonzo. We love you all. God bless you. Abby and Sophia.*

"What a fine letter!" Doctor said. "The best thing to write about is love." He sealed it with warm wax, which he let us press.

"Doctor, I kept a promise to Papa. I told him when the baby came, I'd send him my words in the post. Remember, Soph?"

"Yes," she said. "He said it would be the proudest day of his life when he saw our writing."

Doctor swallowed hard, coughed a bit, and patted our shoulders. "It is a miracle, girls. To write your thoughts. By doing that, you touched your father, same as I am touching you now. You touched home."

That night in bed we squealed and giggled with Maria. A new baby brother made us so proud. Miss Jeanette said we'd each start right away to knit a cap and jacket for Alonzo. Maria would help. We could take it to him at Christmas. This holiday would be the most exciting one ever. We would bring home so many gifts: reading, songs, letters, caps, and love.

∾ 9

Bittersweet Holidays

What wondrous cooking Sarah was doing! We could smell squash pies, corn breads, Indian puddings, and apple tarts, all blending together. We did more sniffing than studying. Ben and I felt hungry most of the time, and Sarah's fine cooking smells gave our stomachs cause to growl. Joe and Sophia were particular eaters, and Maria picked ladylike at her plate. Not Ben and me! Doctor often slipped extra portions to us, saying he was "stoking the furnace." That meant we were growing like a wildfire.

Ben said to Mr. Trencheri, "It must be about time for our state Day of Thanksgiving."

As Doctor returned to do our numbers lesson, he

overheard what Ben said. "Your teachers wouldn't know about Thanksgiving, Ben. It is our American idea to make it a special day."

Mr. Trencheri asked, "You give thanks for the harvest?"

"Yes, and for our freedom," said Doctor. "We cook a great feast here in Boston. Tomorrow you pupils will dress in your best. We will all dine together."

"All of us? But Doctor . . ." I had never sat at table with old Mr. and Mrs. Howe. We hardly sat with Mr. Joseph.

"All of us. Get your number cases ready for subtraction."

❧   ❧   ❧

When the Day of Thanksgiving arrived, Charles and Maria and Sophia and I got our own table against the windows. Young Joe and Ben sat with our teachers and all the Howes at the big table. Sarah loaded the sideboards with roast turkey and goose, along with her oyster stuffing and sweet sauce. As we set pictures of the new places into our heads, Doctor tapped me on the shoulder.

"Abby, please rise. I am holding the Gospel of Saint John. I want you to read a verse for our blessing."

"I may take a while to ponder the big words. . . ."

"You will do your best." Doctor started my finger. I read slowly, but took care to speak it right.

"Amen," said Doctor. "Take your seat, Abby."

From behind me, a man cleared his throat and said, "Father, the girl read the Scripture. It's fair amazing!"

The man was Mr. Joseph.

"I heard her," said old Mr. Howe.

"Humph," said old Mrs. Howe.

"I want to add my blessing," said Doctor proudly. "I thank the Lord for my wonderful pupils and teachers. And for my dear sisters who give us instruction in handiwork and music. And special thanks for my father and stepmother, who allow us to live under their roof. Amen."

I fingered the fine woven cloth, trimmed in lace, and the silver spoons with fancy designs. All we could hear was Sarah, carving at the sideboard.

"Mother, Father," said Mr. Joseph. "Who could imagine Samuel could accomplish such things?"

"The teachers and I have worked hard," said Doctor. "But it is the *pupils* who achieve. They owe you their keep. When they take their places as educated people, they will reward you with their lives."

"Samuel," said Mr. Joseph. "I know you have nothing to thank me for."

"You above all!" Doctor said. "Your labor keeps us."

"I would work no matter what," said Mr. Joseph.

"Let me take the boys to the glass factory for a while on Saturdays. Give them a feel for the ways of machinery. I'd keep them away from harm. What do you say?"

"An excellent idea!"

"And as for the young ladies, perhaps a buggy ride after services? Would that be a nice treat for them?"

"A buggy ride should give them a fine airing, Joseph."

I felt Mr. Joseph turn in his chair and put his hand on my shoulder. It felt huge and heavy. But I did not dislike him anymore. "Miss Abby? Would you be frightened if I cracked the whip on a straightaway? And made old Blaze gallop like the wind?"

"I'd like it above all things!"

"I'll repay you someday," said Doctor in a husky voice.

"Don't talk a fool, Samuel. That goose is getting cold."

So we feasted and talked and laughed among ourselves and tried not to miss our families and their simpler dinners. Although we minded our manners, we never got a kind word from the old Howes. I feared that they might still toss us out before we finished learning.

I thought about how hard the lessons were to learn. Still, they got to be like breathing to me. The words of someone long ago or far away traveled from books to my fingers and into my head. That was reading! My own words came from my head and onto paper to travel to someone else. That was writing! Scales and chords and melodies so fair came from my voice and hands. That was making music! Never did I dream blind people could have such lessons. Seeing lessons, that is what they were. No, I could never give them up. Doctor had won over Mr. Joseph. Would he ever win over his own parents?

The next week, Doctor told us that he decided we must have this public examination at the statehouse. "We will have to prepare. If we put our minds to the task, we can do it."

We read and drilled, we ciphered and wrote, we crocheted and braided, over and over. Mrs. Babcock taught us to walk proud into a room without rolling our heads or looking careless. She showed the boys how to make a proper bow and the girls how to dip into a curtsy. She taught us a vocal so well, we could sing it in our sleep.

"What a troupe of players!" Doctor said. "You will win every heart in the statehouse."

But we had not won the heart of the old Howes. What if we got no money from those legislator fellows? Then we'd be sent home. Perhaps I'd never have school again. I couldn't bear that thought, so I shoved it in a dark corner of my mind.

One morning a knock sounded at the door. We heard Papa greet Doctor Howe in the foyer. Sophia ran and jumped into his arms. I had missed him

so much. When I came to give him a hug, he ex-
claimed how I'd grown even over these four months.
He held my wrists where they stuck out from the
sleeves of my frock. Soon he'd see how much I'd
grown inside my head. I'd tell Mam and Justin and
Richard all about reading books and writing and doing arithmetic on my number case, and learning
crafts, and most of all, having my talent at music. I'd
play those games that Edward loved. And I'd put the
cap and jacket I'd knitted on baby Alonzo and rock
him in my own rocking chair. "Oh, Papa, can we start
back very early in the morning?" I asked. "I can't wait
to be home."

But when the dawn came and I went to the door to
leave, Doctor was there. "Stay well, Abby," he said,
and took my hand.

"And you, Doctor," I said. I felt a pang in my heart
to leave Doctor and his family and our teachers
behind. In a way they had become my family too.

❧   ❧   ❧

The buggy ride home took awful long, for Papa had
to stop every few hours to warm us up and give us hot
drinks. Papa stayed quiet, as he always did, letting us
chatter about all our adventures in Boston. But in his
silence, Papa was keeping something to himself. I
sensed it just from the way he breathed.

"Papa," I finally said as we came near to Andover. "Are you sure Mam is all right?"

"Yes," he said. "Let me drive, girls."

I felt Sophia's mittened hand creep into mine. She sang our vocals softly to herself, humming away her worry.

The chill damp wind had numbed my face when we drove into our yard and put the buggy and horse into the barn. Papa said it was past nightfall. I'd almost forgotten how to find my way to our back door. Familiar smells greeted us when we went inside, the scent of fresh corn bread with simmering split-pea and ham hock soup. Mam and our brothers were not in the kitchen.

While we stood in the mudroom, hanging up our cloaks and bonnets, we stomped the snow off our boots. I kept listening. Why didn't Mam run to us?

Papa came in behind us. "Go to her in the parlor," he said.

The parlor? Although Sophia hurried out of the kitchen to find Mam, I hung back. "Papa, what is it?" Then it came to me. "Did you find out about Alonzo's eyes? You think he's blind? Papa, that's not the end of things for him. We learn so much at the Doctor's school. It's almost like *seeing*. Someday Alonzo can go and see too."

"It's not for me to tell," Papa said softly.

I found Mam holding Sophia on the settee. The parlor was chilly, although I felt a fire in the stove. Mam hugged me close. I brushed her face with my fingertips.

"My Abigail," she said, and gave me a kiss. "All the learning has changed your looks. Made you beautiful as angels."

"Papa said that when you got our letter about Alonzo, you cried from being so proud," I told her.

"I did," she said. Then she caught her breath and let out a sob.

"Don't cry *now*, Mam," Sophia said. "We're here!"

"Yes, my angels. But Alonzo is gone."

That was it. What Papa could not tell us and so kept muffled tightly inside him. I never got to feel his face. The picture of Alonzo the way I imagined him disappeared from my head. My heart felt sick like a knife had cut it open.

"But why?" Sophia demanded. "Why!"

"They called it the influenza. Took a little one from near every family in the Andover congregation. His little chest filled up. . . ." Then Mam squeezed my hand.

"We set his casket before the window when folks came for calling. How many days now, Richard? No flowers this time of year. Folks brought branches of holly. And bittersweet."

Mam cried again.

Then Edward came galloping into the room, with

Richard and Justin behind him. The parlor shook with their steps and warmed with their voices. Edward bumped into my knees with his chubby out-stretched hands. Justin prompted him to call my name. "Say hey, Abby," he said.

I hauled Edward into my lap. His legs had grown some, making him good sized for three years. His curls smelled good like country soap. He squirmed, putting up with my rocking and hugging. I needed him on my lap for as long as he would endure it. Sophia was say-ing sweet things to Mam about God taking Alonzo back to him to heaven. He would be friends with

Jesus. But I couldn't be sweet to Mam. Because I was just so terrible *mad* that the baby got taken away before I even met him. In a way, I was mad at God.

The big boys wanted to hear all about our school in Boston. All the bragging about my lessons I planned to do dried up in my throat. Edward tried to bring me his toys. But I couldn't play games with him. Alonzo would have no toys. He wouldn't go to school in Boston. He wouldn't ever meet Doctor Howe, or even stand at the tollhouse waiting for Providence to enter his life.

I could hardly speak about my reading and writing and math and music. I should have helped Mam with the house. Maybe I could have minded Alonzo or done something to keep him. Mam sent Papa and the boys and Sophia to the kitchen to get some hot soup and bread. Then she came to me. "Most families lose a baby," she said. "It's the hardest part of life."

"I should have helped you," I said. "Do you want me to stay home from the doctor's school?"

Mam hugged me. "I want you to be an educated woman. So your face will keep shining with that light I see."

"I told Doctor about my flashes of light," I said. "He says learning is a light inside us that never goes away."

"He's a wise man," Mam said.

"Mam, did you get mad at God? When he took back Alonzo?"

Mam held my hands tight. "Death brings a terrible pain. But for every pain of being human, we have a joy."

I went to my travel box and took out the cap and jacket I knitted. And I started to cry, letting the anger come out. Mam held me and said, "What fine work you did, Abby. They are teaching you well at the school."

"But it was for our baby."

Mam let me cry some more. "The young Abbots' baby was spared. They are poor and can't afford pretty baby things. Will you put the cap and jacket on their little William?"

I nodded. That would be bitter and it would be sweet.

~ 10

Up at the Statehouse

Our big day dawned cold but crisp. Doctor announced that we would *walk* all the way to the statehouse for our examination. "Briskly walking calms a person's nerves," he told us. I expect this practice worked for him, but Young Joe, Ben, and Sophia and I ended up getting completely agitated. Here is what happened:

Our group marched up Pleasant Street toward the Public Garden. Doctor guided Charles and Maria, who brought samples of our handiwork. Doctor and Charles carried satchels holding our Gospel of Saint John and the *English Stories*. Behind them, Benjamin tapped a cane and held a packet with our writing board and papers. Joe followed Ben, clutching our math slate. Mr. Trencheri led Sophia and me, having us put two fingers in the crook of his arm. Mr. Pringle toted hemp doormats and baskets we'd made in his workshop. Doctor called out descriptions of what was happening so we might follow his booming voice.

"We're passing the Public Garden now," he said. "Remember, I told you that my father once ran a rope factory there? I think we should call it Howe Park."

Across Beacon Street, rich folks lived in large brick houses called "mansions." Doctor said, "Hear the cooks on the stoops? Hear the dairyman on his delivery wagon? Hear the chimney sweep sing?"

As we walked along the Common, I wondered if those white swans Sarah talked about flew away for the winter. Or did they nest there right now? Suddenly I heard some rough-talking boys moving around the edge of the Common near to us.

"Look at the queer children!" one shouted.

"One's got a cane like an old man!"

"One ain't got no eyes. Let's pelt 'em."

A hard cold lump smacked into the back of my cloak. I let out a cry, stumbled, and lost my footing. Mr. Trencheri stood still and grasped me. He asked, "Are you hurt?"

Sophia started in whining and crying, although she was fine.

"What happened, Abby?" Ben called to me.

"I got smacked. Some horrible boys. Probably an ice ball."

"Keep walking straight ahead," Mr. Trencheri said.

"What if the boys chase me?" I was getting agitated now.

"They can just try!" Ben shouted. "Let me at them, Mr. Trencheri. I can whip them."

"Benjamin, we do *not* address cowards!"

Mr. Trencheri was no coward, for sure. He just wanted us not to act low. He was right. Soon we heard those cowards run away.

"I wasn't too scared," I told Ben. "Not with you around."

We arrived at the huge marble steps of the statehouse. "Three steps up," Doctor shouted. "Then ten paces. Turn right. Three more. We are in a high round room called the rotunda."

Doctor's voice boomed and echoed. "Up in the chamber where the general assembly meets, voices may echo also. Don't worry."

When we climbed upstairs, our friend Mr. Mann was waiting. He introduced us to the legislators. Before we could get all nervous again, we were seated in front of the assembly, hearing Mr. Mann talk about the "New England Asylum for the Blind." That was the big name for our little school.

Then he said, "Let me present our director, Doctor Samuel G. Howe." We heard Doctor's chair scrape and his boots stride forward. He did not speak for a while.

"Gentlemen of the Assembly," he said at last. "These are our six blind pupils. They have studied less than six months with our two blind instructors. Because of their handicap, these young people have been denied many experiences enjoyed by the rest of us. But they do have one advantage. Their minds are not often distracted."

Doctor paused, then spoke louder. "Many of you are letting the visual world distract you. If you were blind, you would always pay strict attention to important matters. Gentlemen, the future of these pupils is *important*. So pay attention!"

The gentlemen coughed and shuffled papers and shifted in their chairs. We grinned to hear the Doctor scold the gentlemen like he did us. Doctor then said, "Sophia, reach for my hand."

We knew he'd start with Sophia, because she was so little and sweet to see.

"Miss Sophia Carter is only seven years old," Doctor said. "But she has already gained some skill at reading." Sophia read a few lines from our *English Stories*. "Very good, Sophia," he said as the gentlemen clapped for her.

Doctor said, "Each of these pupils has made astounding progress." Mr. Trencheri made the boys solve mathematics problems on the slate. Joe recited a

poem he learned. Charles sang a solo. Maria showed how well she could write on her raised-line board. Then she held up our handiwork. Each time the gentlemen clapped with surprise.

"Now it is Miss Abby Carter's turn," Doctor said. "I am placing our only other book, the Gospel of Saint John, for her to read. Lest you think we have had these children memorize their parts, call out any chapter and verse. Abby will find it."

I knew the numbers were up in the corner of each page. I prayed I wouldn't get mixed up. Mr. Mann called out, "The start of chapter nine."

I smiled. That was the story of the blind man cured by Jesus. Our favorite one. I read it loud and clear. The gentlemen cried "Bravo!" when I finished.

"Thank you, Abby," Doctor said, and hugged my shoulders. "Through faith and education, our blind will also change. They will be cured of the curse of ignorance."

My other job was locating places on our pasteboard map of the state. When legislators called out towns for me to find, I pointed to each one. We squeezed each other's hands while we sang our vocal. As we made our bows and curtsies, the hall boomed with clapping.

When we stood outside the chamber down the hall, we gave out little shrieks of relief. I heard Doctor pacing about, exclaiming how any man with a heart and a brain *must* vote for us. "By Harry Monmouth," he said, "I will thrash any man who does not!"

All we could do was hold hands and wait. Sophia and Maria were nearly in tears from their shyness and nerves. I felt so proud of us all that my heart pounded with happiness. At last Mr. Mann came striding down the hall.

"Well, Mann?" Doctor shouted.

"It is resolved," Mr. Mann said, "that in this year 1833 it be paid out of the treasury . . . to the Asylum for the Blind . . . the sum of six thousand dollars."

Six thousand was such a big number I couldn't even picture it. Our school would surely go on.

Doctor asked, "When do we get the first payment?"

"Quarterly."

"What do you mean, quarterly?"

"April. Resolutions take time to be approved."

"April! I promised we'd move out this month." Doctor sighed. "Somehow I'll settle it with my family." Then he brightened up. "Tell me, Mann, weren't they brilliant?"

"They opened every closed mind in the house," Mr. Mann said kindly. "Especially Miss Abby. How well she read her Scripture."

"Oh, thanks," I said. "But you gave me the best chapter."

"Then we will have to work together at each

exhibition!" Mr. Mann said, making a joke and patting my arm.

"Mann, that's an idea," Doctor said. "We could do this again. Next time we'll invite the public and ask for donations."

"But you hate this kind of show."

"Yes, I do," said Doctor. "But we need money *now*."

"We will talk of shows later," Mr. Mann said. "If we walk over to the sweetshop on Washington, I will buy everyone some candy. None of us are too old for treats, I presume?"

"I won't hear of it!" Doctor snapped.

"But Howe," Mr. Mann said, "what's wrong?"

"*I* am the director," Doctor said sternly, "so *I* must be the one to buy the candy!"

"Doctor Director," Mr. Mann said, "you have no money."

"You are right." Doctor laughed. "Come now, students, teachers, before Mr. Mann remembers he is almost as poor as I am."

As we made our way to the street, Sophia said to me, "Just think, Abby, a candy cane at Christmas and another only two weeks later! Isn't school the best place?"

"The best." I smiled to myself. Sophia had gotten past her fears and shyness. She had grown up, I thought, even though her wrists didn't yet stick out of her sleeves.

When we got back to Doctor's house, chilled and sticky from the candy, the doctor's sisters were waiting. They cheered and clapped when they heard the good news about the vote. Mrs. Babcock, the only one with the knack for teasing Doctor, said, "I suppose you will be taking rooms at the Tremont House, now that you are so wealthy."

The other sisters giggled. But Doctor did not laugh. "We do not get the first payment until April."

"Oh, dear," said Miss Jeanette. "You told our stepmother . . ."

"I know. I'd better tell her the truth."

As we got herded back to the kitchen to shed our cloaks and get warm by the stove, I heard Mrs. Babcock whisper, "Samuel, she will insist on sending them home."

"I will beg Father. He ran a factory. He will remember that machines and minds should not be shut down when they have begun to produce. He will take my side."

We heard him march down the hall to the old Howes' study. He was a man over thirty years old. Yet he humbled himself and begged to keep us. Doctor spent so long talking to the old Howes that we had an early supper alone. We were sent up to bed without knowing our fate.

At breakfast we buzzed among ourselves. Would the Howes put us out? Would the state money be enough to buy us a school? Were the lessons over forever? Such worries made notions pop into my head. I said to the others, "We could do more chores for Cook Sarah. Sophia and Ben and I are used to chores at home. Then the Howes wouldn't mind us. Maria could do mending for them. Charles might polish the silver. And Young Joe . . ."

I got so excited that my ideas blurred the picture of the breakfast table in my mind. I swung my hand, and my cider went flying. Sophia and Maria let out shrieks, and Sarah came running. As I felt the cider creep across the cloth, I knew I'd picked the worst time to make a mess. How did I think I was so smart that I could save the school?

I hung my head down and cried.

~ 11
I Am Really Blind!

Like a swollen creek, my tears kept overflowing. Maybe it was due to getting slopped by my cider, but Sophia and Maria started sobbing with me. Crying can be as catching as the croup. Joe, who had a sore throat, coughed.

Cook Sarah grumbled, "Lord have mercy! Not a housekeeper in Boston would put up with what befalls me. I've gone from five fine grown folks to twelve in an asylum. Along with teachers in my kitchen, visitors in the parlor, and now all this dirty linen and weeping . . . and nary a raise in wages."

At that moment we heard Doctor's boots striding quickly into the dining room.

"Oh, Doctor Howe." Sarah jumped. "We thought you'd gone into the city, so we'd started without. Now there's such a commotion."

"Sarah, I know you are overworked. But you will discuss it with *me*, not the pupils. Please wait in the kitchen." We could sense Doctor's temper crackling.

"Yes, sir." Sarah stomped off.

Doctor walked slowly around the table. "Joe, sip your honeyed tea for that cough. Maria, what's upset you?"

"I'm all right, Doctor," she said, swallowing her tears.

"Sophia? Why were you crying?"

"Because Abby was. And she hardly ever does."

"So it comes to you, Abby. Wipe your face."

Doctor put his hand on my shoulder. The sharp edge was gone from his voice. He spoke with the comfortable sound we often leaned on. So I told him, "Instead of thinking of how to make things better, I made it worse. I ruined a tablecloth. No wonder your folks want us gone."

"Years ago there were six children in this house," Doctor said. "Including my brother who is at sea. My father remembers. So he has awarded us more time. Our school will stay here through the spring."

"Even though we make a lot of work?" I asked.

"Yes. Even then."

"But Sarah needs more wages," Sophia said.

"These are worries of grown folks. Your job is . . . ?"

We replied together: "To be good students."

"Correct. Abby, do you feel better now?"

"I do, so long as you say we'll have school."

Doctor quickly ate his muffin and gulped his tea. "I am off to town to talk to our trustees. Work hard, pupils."

As Doctor dashed out, Mr. Trencheri and Mr. Pringle arrived to begin lessons. Ben said to Mr. Pringle, "Can't we sell our mats and wood baskets? Doctor needs money for the school."

"I know, lad. But you're not good enough yet for selling. Someday down the road, you will be."

Ben wanted to be a craftsman. Maria wanted to keep a house. Once I figured we'd never leave the farm. Now we had *choices*. I could read and write and play and sing! My new notion of being a music teacher might even happen. It made your head spin to have these choices. If we kept having lessons, blind people could do just about anything, couldn't we? Like I kept telling Sophia, so long as we could have school, we could have dreams.

Doctor didn't return until music class that night. Mrs. Babcock was teaching us the G scale. We had already learned the C and the D. As we sang, he burst through the door.

"Maria, excuse me," Doctor said to his sister. "But I must tell you all the good news. The trustees got together enough money to rent the new Masonic Temple for one night."

"My, Samuel, that's the grand new hall, isn't it?"

"Yes, and we must fill it. My friends at the news-papers will give us free advertising."

"Fill it for what?" Mrs. Babcock asked.

"Why, for our public examination."

"Oh. Samuel, you look very tired."

"Not at all," he said firmly. "On with music class. We must sound marvelous by February sixth."

Then Doctor started to cough even worse than Joe. When he walked out of the room, he sounded unsteady.

"Is Doctor sick?" I asked Mrs. Babcock.

"He runs night and day," she said. "But he always tells us, *I* am the doctor. We are not to worry."

"We could ask Doctor Fisher to thump his chest," Joe said. "Like he does mine."

"My dears," said Mrs. Babcock, "there is no better doctor than ours. Now back to the G scale. Sophia?"

And Soph ran up the notes, do-re-mi, clear as a warbler.

❧   ❧   ❧

We had only a week to polish up for this new "examination." The plan was to do the same readings

and math problems and songs we did for the legislators. Doctor would make a begging speech. Then the
folks at this temple would stuff baskets with money.
We would pay the old Howes and Sarah what we
owed them. What a grand plan, we thought.

When our big night came, we packed into Mr.
Joseph's carriage, while Doctor rode his stallion. The
night air was so damp and raw that I could hardly
breathe in deep. In truth, I felt weak and feverish all
the night before. I decided it was from the excitement.
Since Doctor and Joe had stopped coughing, I wasn't
going to be the one who got sick. So I told no one.

"By the devil, it's cold as sin!" Mr. Joseph shouted
as he cracked the whip over Blaze. "Children, keep
those fur robes pulled up over you."

"Do you think anyone will come to see us in this
cold?" Ben wondered out loud. "I wouldn't!"

As Mr. Joseph drove the carriage up to the Masonic
Temple door, he said, "You are a sensible boy, Benjamin. But it appears plenty of folks have more curi-
osity than brains. There's a mob already here."

While we were taken inside, loud mumbling and
shuffling all around us made me tremble. Sophia
squeezed my hand so tight it ached. It seemed like no
matter where she touched me, it hurt. Doctor took
our cloaks and bonnets, then set us in a row of chairs
up on a stage.

"Do this examination just as we have practiced it," he told us. "The same order as we used at the statehouse."

Maria said, "It sounds like hundreds of people."

"Yes," said Doctor. "All manner and variety. But listen to me, and you shall win every heart."

Except, somehow, things went badly. This crowd was full of rowdy, coarse folks. Doctor had to outshout them to introduce us. When Sophia stood to do her first reading from the *English Stories*, she spoke in such a tiny voice, no one heard her. Ben solved his problems on his number case, but some fellows from the back kept yelling, "We can't see nothing from here, and we ain't even blind!"

Then it was my turn. I was truly shaky now and not just from excitement. I forgot all my lessons from Mrs. Babcock about holding my head up straight and walking ladylike. Instead I fell back in my old careless habits and rolled my head and eyeballs.

People began to yell at us:

" 'Tis a fake! I seen that gal turn her head and look around. She can see!"

"She's staring straight at me!"

"Sure, 'tis fakery. How else could blind youngsters read and figure when they been idiots in the past?"

"Hey, Doctor, you're a sham!"

"You're putting on a show to get our money."

"Quackery! They can *all* see!"

I groped for Doctor, but I couldn't reach him. From behind me, I heard Sophia start to whine, "Abbeee . . . ," and fall to weeping. Maria tried to hush her. I started to shake so badly I could hardly stand.

For the first time since we left home, I wanted to cry from fear. This was much worse than my first night away or when the boys by the Common hit me with ice balls. This time I felt like a lost thing. Who could protect us from this many angry people?

I heard a great pounding on the table that held our books. Doctor's fist was trying for order. Then he grabbed my hand.

"Don't fear, Abby, I would never let those fools near you. Fakers, by God!"

"If only they could be blind for one day," I said. "Like you did with your blindfold. Then they'd know!"

Suddenly Doctor hugged me hard around the shoulders. "Stop this trembling," he said. "You have hit on it!"

"I did?"

"Yes! We shall show them what it is to be blind."

Doctor placed both my hands on our Gospel of Saint John. Then he yelled in his most powerful booming way, "Ladies and gentlemen! Will six of you lend me your kerchiefs?"

The folks stopped shouting but kept mumbling. An old man came to our stage and said, "Take mine, Doctor Howe. I am Colonel Thomas Perkins."

"I thank you, Colonel. And these others . . . ?"

"They belong to my daughter Mary Ann and her husband, Mr. Cary. We all have great faith in you."

Then we heard the familiar voice of our friend Doctor Fisher: "Here, Howe. Take mine too."

Soon the crowd quieted and watched. Doctor wrapped a folded kerchief around my eyes and tied it. "You are too clever for them, Abby," he said. "They can't believe what they see. So I am blindfolding you." He turned and did the same to Sophia, Ben, Joe, and Maria and Charles. Then he stood beside me at the table and told the crowd, "Jesus said: Blessed are they who have not seen, yet they have believed. My pupils cannot see as you and I do. You who can see will be made to believe."

I said in a quavery voice, "I will read from the Gospel of Saint John. Please call out a chapter?"

And I heard from the back of the hall the well-known voice of our friend Mr. Mann: "The start of chapter nine."

I smiled. As I read the story, I heard someone say, "The girl can read without seeing—that is fair amazing!"

I finished reading about Jesus' miracle.

"Oooh," ladies cried. "It *is* a miracle."

The crowd clapped for us like thunder. After our final vocal and bows, we clung to Doctor. This rowdy bunch roared such approval, the floor shook with their stomps and cheers.

Doctor told us, "We will never be called fakers again. From now on, when we are in public, we will cover our eyes. Satin eye bands for the girls, smoked glasses for the boys."

After all the baskets full of money were brought to the table, the old man named Perkins came back. With each pace his walking stick hit the floor like a third leg. He smelled of fine woolens and barley-water cologne.

"You young people sold 'em," he said to us. "And you, Doctor. Amazing progress with these unfortunates."

"Thank you for your kerchiefs. I'll launder them."

"Keep 'em, Doctor. Now how do you plan to fund your asylum once you've done these shows to death?"

"The legislature voted to give us six thousand a year. Starting in April."

"Fine. But that will not buy you a building, support a staff, twenty pupils, supplies, equipment."

"No. But we have been crowding my father out of his own house since September."

"So Joseph Howe has put you all up? Commendable.

Don't make a move, Doctor, until I see what I can do to help. Good evening to you all."

And off he went, step-step-thump, with his stick. As Doctor and Mr. Joseph bundled us up in our cloaks, Doctor said, "Do you remember him, Joseph? From when we were boys on Pearl Street? Old Colonel Perkins himself!"

"Yes, the king of the China trade," said Mr. Joseph.

I tried to walk, but my knees just buckled. My face flared hot, like I'd stuck it in the oven. My head spun inside as I felt myself getting picked up off my feet.

"Abby, what's the matter?" Mr. Joseph asked. "Samuel, look close at the girl!"

Doctor pressed his hands to my cheeks. "She has fever."

"No," I whispered.

"Why didn't you tell me?"

"The show. I was the star."

"God forgive me. Joseph, get the carriage, man!"

Doctor ran with me in his arms and climbed into the frigid carriage. I started to giggle, like you might do in a dream. Because I was still wearing the Colonel's kerchief. I clung to Doctor, giggling as my teeth chattered. My laughter banged around inside my head.

"It's freezing and I am burning." I giggled to

Doctor. "It's night and I am blindfolded . . . and I am really blind!"

"Oh, Lord," Doctor said, holding me tightly. "Joseph, crack that whip!"

As we raced along Tremont Street, I felt Doctor's arms tremble. For the first time since I knew him, I believe he was the one who was afraid.

❧ 12
Touching the Light

I went in and out the window.

That's what it feels like when you have the fever. You fly through space with visions of things exploding. Then you sail back in where your body is lying in bed. You hear Doctor Howe and Doctor Fisher talking about medicines. Gentle hands and cool cloths press on your skin. You don't recall the time. You call for your mother. Then you fly again.

Once in a dream I was choking. I couldn't get enough air to cough. Then I sailed back in the window and sat up straight in bed. My eyes flew wide open as I coughed. Then I saw it: a flash of light.

"Doctor? I see light."

"I'm holding the brightest oil lamp we have. Where is it?"

I reached out my finger, slowly, toward the glowing place, where it was warm and bright. "There." My finger felt a sharp pain. "It's the lamp!"

"Hold still," said Doctor. "Let me look into your eyes."

He held the lamp so close, my nose got hot. But the glow started to fade. Slowly the nothingness came back.

"It's gone," I said. "But I touched the light, didn't I?"

"Yes," Doctor said. "You surely did. Now try to sleep."

I tried. But my coughing and thrashing kept me half awake. Then I had a beautiful dream: I was a huge bird, maybe a black swan, flying high in the sky. I could see. Below me was our whole state of Massachusetts like it was on our twine map. Then I looked up—and saw the glorious sun.

❧   ❧   ❧

After my fever broke, Doctor kept me in bed for days. All I could do was some crocheting with Miss Jeanette, who nursed me. I missed lessons so much. At recess time I could hear Sophia and Joe and Ben laughing in the garden below, making snow people. How I longed to join them. Each night Doctor sat in my room with the lamp to be sure I didn't "wander in dreamland." I think he wanted to see if I sat up again and touched the light.

Finally I came down to the breakfast table. Everyone made a fuss over me. I remembered where all things were set. But my stomach forgot how to eat a meal. I had to coax it. That afternoon, I was stretched on the parlor settee with Miss Jeanette, crocheting. Maria was helping Sophia learn to knit. Doctor and Mr. Trencheri were in the dining room, giving the math and writing lessons to the boys. The door knocker sounded. As Miss Jeanette answered the knock, a cold wind poured into the parlor. I had almost forgotten how the winter world felt.

"Is Doctor Samuel Howe in?" a man asked her.

"Yes, he is," said Miss Jeanette.

"I am Colonel Perkins's footman. Please present his calling card, ma'am. He's waiting outside."

Miss Jeanette returned through the parlor and

opened the door to the dining room. "Samuel," she called. "See who is here!"

Doctor rushed in. "Settle the girls in the dining room."

"Yes, Samuel," said Miss Jeanette as she swooshed us out of the parlor. We sat around the big table and tried to join in math and writing. But our minds danced with notions of why the Colonel called. To see another show? To buy our handicrafts? To give us more kerchiefs?

We didn't even come close to guessing.

After a while, the doors to the dining room were thrown open. Doctor shouted, "Father, Mother, come in here! The man who has traded it all, Chinese teas and spices and silks, wants to trade in his house!"

We had no idea what Doctor was raving about. I got scared—what if he had the fever now?

Soon we heard the old Howes walk in. "Samuel, what did the Colonel want?" old Mr. Howe asked.

"Father, you must remember the Colonel's mansion from when we lived on Pearl Street. Now he is building a new one in Temple Place. And he wants to give *us* the one on Pearl Street!"

"Give it to *you*?" old Mrs. Howe asked.

"Yes! As a school for the blind," Doctor said.

"What is his mansion like, Doctor?" I asked.

"Very grand, Abby. Three full floors, a finished cellar, a lovely garden. I recall large rooms over the carriage house. That should do for the staff. You pupils, and the fourteen to come, will fit nicely."

Old Mr. Howe said, "That's a mighty fine offer. But Perkins must know you can't run such property on your money from the state."

"He has wisely looked to the future. He wants funds raised to keep up the buildings. He mentioned fifty thousand dollars."

Old Mrs. Howe said, "Fine chance of that happening."

"We *shall* raise it!" Doctor insisted. "Now, excuse us please. We have lessons."

That was that. We were not allowed to discuss raising this huge amount of money. Doctor said, "Teachers must teach, and pupils must learn. *I* will worry about money."

Our music class that night was brief, because Mrs. Babcock had "a ladies' engagement." As a widow, it was time for her to start going to ladies' homes and meeting people. So we were sent to bed early. Still, we were eager to talk. Joe and Ben crept up the back stairs to our floor. They called to us girls, and we met them at the end of the chilly hall, our shawls pulled tightly.

"How do you think we can get that fifty thousand?" Joe asked. "Keep doing our 'examination'?"

Ben snorted. "Everybody in Boston would have to stuff money in our basket!"

"I want to have school in the mansion," said Sophia. She liked the sound of that word.

"We'll end up in some smelly old boardinghouse," said Ben.

"I don't care," I said. "As long as we have school."

"We could go home, Abby," Soph said. "We learned to read some now."

"We *have* to keep school going. We have so many more lessons to learn. And other blind children are waiting to come."

"Abby's right," said Maria. "But it's too much for us, raising this money. We'd best leave it to Doctor."

We crept back to our beds and huddled under the quilts. Papa always said, "The Lord helps those who help themselves." I knew if I thought hard enough, I'd get a good idea to help Doctor.

☙   ☙   ☙

As the days passed, we waited for Doctor to announce his plan to get fifty thousand dollars. He never did. We waited for Mr. Mann and the trustees to arrive with their plan. But they never did either. The only thing that arrived daily was old Mr. Howe, who rode through every kind of weather to bring home the mail. Among the Doctor's letters came a packet from Salem, a town north of Boston. He shared it with us as we set up the dining room table for dinner.

"Here's a nice letter from the pastor of the Salem Congregational Church, pupils. The ladies want to help you keep your school. So they got up a little fair."

"Salem's next to my town," Ben said.

"Yes, Ben. The Marblehead ladies are having their own table of things to sell. Perhaps your relatives are behind it."

"What will they sell at this fair?" I asked.

"Says here, ladies' things, baby clothes, dolls,

sewing bags, even some paintings. I wonder how much they will sell?"

"At Mum's church, they like to have a contest," Ben said, "to see whose table sells the most. But friendlylike."

Doctor said, "Yes, ladies do love a bit of friendly competition."

We went on with our chores. Ben and Charles loaded the stove with wood. Maria and I set the forks, and Sophia did the napkins. Suddenly I had one of those ideas like a flash of light.

"Doctor, we all like to have contests," I said. "What if every church in Boston had a fair and tried to sell the most? And what if they all gave us what they earned?"

The Doctor came over to me. "A fair throughout the city? It has never been done. Abby, what a splendid idea!"

"Doctor, do you think the entire city would work for our school?" Maria asked. "Most haven't even heard of us."

"You are right," Doctor said. "Which means we must get the most important ladies to head this fair. Ladies like Madame Perkins herself, the Colonel's wife!"

"If she is as kind as her husband, she will," I said.

"By Harry Monmouth, I shall ask her myself. This

very evening. Tell Cook Sarah not to wait dinner for me."

Doctor dashed away, slamming the door so it shook the house.

The Doctor's visit with Madame Perkins was a big success. The next day at breakfast he announced that my idea caught her fancy. Madame and her daughters decided they would head up the biggest fair ever seen in Boston. They would rent a large hall, run the fair for a week, and call it the May Fair for the Blind. Every church would have a table of wonderful goods to sell.

I was starting to think quite a bit of myself. First my Scripture readings had impressed everybody at our examinations. As Mr. Mann said, I won people over. Now I had the best idea of the city fair. Sophia, I'll admit, never seemed jealous of me.

Then things changed. One day while we were talking about American history with Mr. Trencheri, a strange gentleman arrived at the house. Doctor brought him into the dining room to meet us.

"This is Chester Harding, the painter."

We did not know exactly what a painter was.

"He will paint one of you students," Doctor said, "to sell at the fair. Should bring a goodly sum."

I felt Sophia cling to me. She was wary of this gentleman.

"Tell the little one to step forward," said Mr. Harding.

"You may ask her yourself," Doctor said. "Her name is Sophia Carter, and she hears very well."

The gentleman asked Sophia to come with him. She still clung to me. "What is he going to do to me?"

"Nothing bad," I said, knowing Doctor would not permit it.

Doctor took Sophia's hand from mine. He patted my head. "Couldn't you paint both sisters?"

"Not enough time. And the little one is so sweet to see."

I'd heard that often enough. Something about Sophia was pleasing to sighted people. I could beat her at lessons and contests, but not in looks. That started to sting me.

"Let me explain what Mr. Harding will do," Doctor said to all of us. "He will look at Sophia carefully. He will take a plain piece of canvas and creamy colored liquids we call paints. He will make the image of Sophia go from his eyes through his paintbrush. And Sophia will appear on the canvas."

That did sound magical. It was hard enough for us to draw our letters on our writing slate. This man could draw all of Sophia on his canvas.

"Sophia will grow up to be a lovely woman," Doctor said. "But after the painting of her dries, it will never change. Sophia will stay young and sweet forever."

That was the start of my jealousy, which I kept to myself.

During April, we gave up having lessons after luncheon. Constant commotion of ladies at work filled the house. Mr. Trencheri and Mr. Pringle helped us do better crafts, in hopes that the best ones could be sold at the fair. My work was deemed to be good enough. All Soph could do was crochet baby stockings. Most weren't worth selling, I'm afraid.

One morning a lady friend of Mrs. Babcock's came with her to the house. She had a dress of satin with bows on each shoulder. They put it on Sophia. "Oh, how sweet to see!" said the lady. "Now she is ready to sit for Mr. Harding."

"Abby must come with me to Mr. Harding," Sophia insisted.

"I shall bring you," said Mrs. Babcock.

"No, Abbeeee!" Sophia cried.

Doctor said it was best I go along to see that Sophia behaved herself. Sophia got to wear the fancy dress and hold a rose. I got to be her hired girl. Thank you, I liked that not!

While we were driving Sophia to Mr. Harding's in a hackney, Mrs. Babcock told us that she and Miss

Jeanette and Miss Elizabeth were in charge of the cake and iced-cream table at the fair. Their lady friends all promised to bring cakes, sweets, lemonade, and supplies of iced cream. They would take turns selling the treats.

"I'll bet you win the prize," I told her. "For the Friendly Competition. You will win over all the other tables."

Mrs. Babcock laughed. "From what I hear, there will be goods on those other tables costing a thousand times more than a plate of cake. But we will do our part."

"Please let me help you. I can serve cake neatly."

"I am sure. But many ladies are eager to help in this cause."

I wasn't fooled. They didn't want to bother with me. I was too young and blind. As it turned out, getting painted was dull work for Sophia. Mr. Harding kept saying "chin up" and "hold still." Mrs. Babcock was not allowed to talk out loud—Mr. Harding's rule—so she could not tell me what was happening. The paints stunk, and I got a headache. We had to come back three times. Finally the painting of Sophia was finished.

"It should bring in a hundred dollars," Mr. Harding said.

"Because I'm so sweet to see?" Sophia asked.

"Partly," he said. "But it's mainly because *I* painted you."

On the way home in the hackney, Sophia poked me. "I'm going to bring lots of money at the fair," she said.

At that, my jealousy truly started to smolder.

❧ 13
How the Fair Was Fair

I don't know how it happened, but everyone got to be more important than I was at the New England Asylum for the Blind. First Doctor decided that Sophia would go to the fair when they put her painting up for sale. Seeing her would please the people and make them bid more money. Sophia went on about this until I could scream. Then, after pestering Mrs. Babcock near to death, Joe got her permission to help at the fair. He would stand by her table and cry, "Cakes and cream!" How he gloated over this important job. Maria and Ben kept quiet in front of me to be polite. Still, I heard Mr. Pringle say that their handiwork was so good, they could have their own space at a table. Mine was not exactly mentioned.

It was not fair. One evening during kitchen chores, I gave Sophia a pinch for bragging. She yowled like a scalded cat. Joe was scooping out the hearth. "You're just jealous, Abby," he said.

"You be quiet, or I'll shove you in the ashes!" I said.

"I'll call the doctor on the lot of you," Cook Sarah said.

However, Doctor was just coming in from the stable and heard us. "Finish your chores," he said loudly. "Then I will see Miss Abigail in her room."

When Doctor left, Sophia jeered at me, "You'll get a punishment."

So I said the scariest thing I could to her: "When you go to the fair to sell your painting, there will be this huge mob. And you'll get lost!"

It did not make me feel much relieved to hear her whimpering when I went up to meet Doctor in our hall. As we sat together on my bed, he reminded me that quarreling was forbidden.

"I know. Sorry, sir."

"What is the reason for having the May Fair?"

"Why, to sell lots of goods and cakes and have a grand time."

"Yes, but what is the final reason?"

"Oh. To make enough money to keep Colonel Perkins's mansion."

"Yes, but the reason beyond that?"

"You mean, to keep our school going?"

"Yes. And for whom do we do this?"

"For us."

"I think you have been so busy quarreling that you forgot your baby brother."

"Alonzo is dead," I said without thinking.

"Yes, but Edward is alive and waiting his chance."

Poor little Edward with his chubby knees and thick curls. I had let him slip from my head while I thought about myself. That hot painful wave that means you might cry rose up in me. "I'm so sorry," I whispered.

"We are all at fault," Doctor said, and patted my shoulder. "Folks are so swept up in the fair, they have forgotten its meaning. For picking a quarrel with Sophia and Joe, you will spend the evening alone in your room." He walked to the hall, then stopped. "Forgive us, Abby, for making you actors instead of students."

He left me alone that night to ponder his words.

Next week Doctor introduced us to a young lady in the parlor. As she took my hand, I felt her tiny fingers covered with lacy gloves. "This is Miss Cornelia Walter, daughter of the newspaper editor. She has a special job at our fair."

I curtsied but did not really care, since I had no job at the fair myself. "I'm Abigail Carter," I said.

Miss Cornelia stroked my hair. She smelled like roses. "Miss Abby, I am going to impersonate Flora, the goddess of flowers, and stand under a bower. I will dress in Flora's robe and sell fresh flowers."

"I'd buy them all if I could," I told her. "I love flowers."

Miss Cornelia laughed lightly, like a song, and said, "If you are willing to stand beside me and portray Flora's handmaid, I believe we will sell every blossom. The gentlemen will be smitten. What do you say?"

"I would do my best!"

"You will sell just a few hours a day," Doctor said. "So you ladies won't wilt before the flowers. But it will be tiring."

"May I have a robe like Flora's and have my hair done up?"

"Yes, indeed," said Miss Cornelia. "You are a performer at heart. Farewell, my handmaid."

I curtsied and said good-bye. Doctor showed Miss Cornelia out, then came to find me.

"Are you happier now?" he asked me. "About the fair?"

How could he know I felt the fair wasn't fair? "I just want to raise money like all the others," I told him.

"Don't let any of this swell your head. You are just our Abby, a good daughter and sister, and a good pupil and friend."

I beamed at him. Then I remembered I had not

been such a good sister. "Doctor, about Sophia. She's scared to go to the fair. Too many strangers. Could the Goddess Flora have two handmaids? Soph could hold on to my robe. And look sweet to see."

Doctor patted my shoulder, the way he did when he was proud. "Sighted people are used to looking for sweetness on the outside. I am trying to learn to be like you, and look for sweetness on the inside."

I ran to find Sophia and tell her the exciting news.

❧   ❧   ❧

As we climbed to the upper chamber of Faneuil Hall, I took a deep sniff and smelled a hundred kinds of fish. They were sold in the lower stalls. We pupils, led by Doctor and Mrs. Babcock, were going to be the first guests at the May Fair for the Blind.

As we entered the Grand Hall, the air took on a new fragrance. "We're in the piney forest," I said. "Just like behind our pond at home. How can it be?"

"Because someone has brought the forest to Faneuil!" said Mrs. Babcock. "Rows of tall living ever-greens and thick pine garlands! Sales tables decked with greens and flowers. Oh, and in the center they have set up a true Maypole strung with every color of ribbon! Around it is a grand table with the loveliest goods to sell. Let me put your hands on it. . . ."

As we felt the pole and its ribbons, I heard a familiar sound. "They left the birds in those evergreens."

"No." Mrs. Babcock laughed. "They have put them in gilded cages. Behind the trees are tall mirrors. Silk banners hang from the galleries. Crystal lamps are all around. It's a wonderland!"

Slowly we walked around the hall, trying to picture the beauty of these decorations. Then Doctor called to his sister, "How do you like your cake and iced-cream table?"

Grabbing our hands, Mrs. Babcock fairly skipped across the floor. "It has a brocade cloth and silky banners, and a great cut-glass lemonade bowl, and silver cake trays. It's perfect."

We had never heard Mrs. Babcock act giddy before. Sophia and I wandered through the rest of the hall, feeling our way from table to table. Then we heard someone call to us. "Hello, Abby and Sophia. It's Elizabeth Peabody. My sister and I called on you with Mr. Mann?"

"Oh yes," I said. "How are you?"

"Fine, my dears. And here is Miss Mary. We are selling many books. Feel the covers. Some titles have raised letters."

"It says *Pil . . . grim's Pro . . . gress.*"

"That's it, Abby."

But when I opened the book, the pages were slick

and barren. I couldn't read a word. These books were for sighted people. They were closed as coffins to me.

"Don't frown," said Miss Elizabeth. "Someday Doctor Howe will print many books for you on a special press."

"Where is this special press?"

"Doctor Howe must invent it," said Miss Mary. "He and Mr. Mann are trying to find a way to get the money."

Money again! I wanted books under my fingers, *now!* Then I heard Doctor's voice. "What is Doctor doing?" I asked.

"Passing among the ladies setting up their tables," said Miss Mary. "He certainly causes a stir!"

"He's the handsomest man in Boston," Miss Elizabeth added.

"Oh, Elizabeth," said Miss Mary in a reproving way.

"What does he look like?" I asked Miss E.

"Why, Mary, they have a right to know," said Miss E. "He is well turned out in a tan topcoat and blue weskit. He is tall as a soldier and clean-shaven. He wears his hair short. It is wavy and ebony black."

Like the black swan? "I think we better find Flora's Bower," I said. So Miss Mary led us between the tables and boxes until we found ourselves by a raised stage.

"The bower is an arch over your heads, trimmed in hemlock branches," said Miss M. "Men are decorating it with blossoms and banners. I'll leave you here. Good-bye for now."

"Thanks, Miss Mary."

Sophia and I perched on the stage. Among all the voices and laughter, I didn't hear Miss Cornelia, who would be Flora. Another lady with a deep musical voice leaned close to us. "Are you Cornelia's handmaids?"

"Yes, ma'am."

"I am Sybil the Fate Lady," she said. "I have a table where I'll deal the cards."

"Deal the cards?" Sophia said. "What are cards?"

We edged over until we were by the Fate Lady's table and could feel the pieces of cardboard. "Here, touch my hands," she said. Her slim fingers were covered in rings. She handed each of us one of the cardboards. "People will pay me to tell their fate as I turn up the cards."

Sophia and I didn't know what she meant, but we liked her interesting and mysterious voice. Then we heard laughter like a song and felt tiny hands that smelled of roses.

"I see you girls have met the Fate Lady," said Miss Cornelia. "She is *really* Miss Louisa Adams under her gypsy scarves."

"How d'you do, ma'am," I said. "I mean, Miss Sybil. No, I mean, Miss Louisa."

The Fate Lady said, "Don't be confused. At the fair, we all have a part to play. Mine is to read the cards. They help me to see people's past, present, and future. Of course, you must have some faith in them."

"Louisa, don't tease the girls," said Miss Cornelia, who was Flora. "It's only a game."

"Abby, come feel my face and costume," offered Miss Louisa.

"We aren't to feel folks," I said.

"Doctor Howe says it's not proper," said Sophia.

"Does he? I am permitting it now."

Sophia and I leaned close to the Fate Lady as she placed our hands on her face. She had smooth skin, bangles on her earlobes, and thick curls popping out from under her scarves. She wore fringed silky shawls and beaded necklaces. As I felt her, she whispered to me, "On the last day of the fair, I shall read your fate in the cards."

"You mean you can see things coming?"

"Sometimes," she said. My finger traced her smile.

"Abby! Sophia!"

We jumped like grasshoppers at the sound of Doctor's voice.

"Are you girls being forward?"

"Doctor Howe, the Fate Lady is at fault. Because I can see all, I wanted the girls to see also."

Doctor cleared his throat. "Miss Adams, I—that

is, we—try to keep the pupils . . . they must never be forward."

"They were most polite," said the Fate Lady. "Cornelia and I are very glad to have their company."

"Thank you, Miss Adams. I leave them in your lovely hands."

With that, Doctor went off to the other tables.

Sophia and I sat on the stage as Miss Cornelia told the men where to place her buckets of flowers. Miss Jeanette put on our robes, fussed with our hair, and got us to eat our butterbread and dried fruit. The salesladies in the hall settled in their places. We heard Doctor walking round and round, followed by a trail of ladies' giggles. Then the clock struck one.

"Ready, my handmaids?" asked Miss Cornelia. "Abby, you will draw flowers from the bucket on my right. Sophia, sit on Abby's right. Take a deep breath, girls. The fair begins!"

❦ 14
Looking Forward and
Traveling Back

The doors flew open, and a herd of humans stampeded toward us. At first it was distracting to have Sophia tugging on my robe, but I kept my mind on my job. The Goddess Flora was depending on me.

"Flora, the queen of May, welcomes you," said Miss Cornelia. "What will I be offered for this one perfect rose?"

Two dollars, five dollars, eight dollars, ten!

That's how we did it, Flora and her handmaids. Gentlemen shouted their bids each time I handed Miss Cornelia another bouquet. She talked so familiar to men she hardly knew. Finally an old lady yelled, "Cornelia Walter, you are too bold!"

"We must be bold here in the Forest of Enchantment," said Flora. "We spare no means to help these sweet blind children."

The old lady could not answer back to that.

By the fifth day, many gentlemen were winning the bouquets, paying their money, and handing the flowers right back to Miss Cornelia. A Mr. Richards came every day.

"This is our final bid," Miss Cornelia said. "Who will buy this one perfect branch of crimson gladiolus?"

"Miss Walter, I must have it," said the gentleman.

"Mr. Richards, are you not quite out of money?" Miss Cornelia laughed. "You have bid so many times."

"I'd give all I have to win fair Flora's heart."

All the other bidders stopped. The whole hall got quiet.

"Very well, Mr. Richards," said Miss Cornelia. "What is your bid for this floral treasure?"

"Twenty-five dollars."

Everybody gasped. That was the highest bid ever.

Miss Cornelia did not quit. "Will no other bidder come forth? For this most worthy cause?"

Sophia and I knew she was pointing at us.

"Yes," said another man. "I will bid thirty. But *you* must pass me the branch, Miss Walter."

Everyone went "Ah."

"Then give it over, Mr. Richards," said Flora. And she passed it to the other man.

"I will bid fifty dollars, Miss Walter! Only to have the pleasure of your placing it in my hand."

More "ahs" echoed through the hall.

"Then, Mr. Richards, the pleasure is yours."

"I am cleaned out," said the other man.

"I am your humble servant," said Mr. Richards. "To Flora and her handmaids, I present this perfect branch, along with my heart."

Everyone started clapping and cheering. I don't know what happened after that between Miss Cornelia and Mr. Richards. But somehow *I* ended up getting the gladiolus. Then the bidding was announced for the painting of Sophia. Mr. Harding and Doctor took her away, leaving me sitting on the bower beside the Fate Lady.

"They have placed Sophia upon a table where the painting is displayed," said Miss Louisa.

"Does she look scared?" I asked.

"A bit. But Doctor Howe holds her hand."

We heard a man call out, "One hundred dollars in gold!" Since no one outbid him, he must have won the painting. "Abby," said Miss Louisa, "Doctor is leading Sophia to the cake table. Would you like me to tell your fate?"

This would be my one chance to have a secret. I sat across from her and she held my hands. We let a warm feeling pass between us. Then she laid my hands on her table.

"I am turning up three cards for you," she said. "The first card tells about your past. It shows a woman balancing fire in her torch with water in her glass. Once you had trouble staying in balance. You had plenty to do with your body, but not enough use for your mind."

"You mean before I had lessons," I said.

"The second card is for your present," said the Fate Lady. "It shows a full chalice of water. It tells me that now you are growing in your mind and creative talent. You are learning to write and sing. Someday you will use this creative talent."

I thought about my dream to be a teacher and musician. "The third card is for your future. It shows four small circles with stars in them, placed in a square. This means your future is in order. You will be secure."

"You mean we'll get the mansion for our school?"

"It means many things. Probably that you will finish school and be able to earn a living. But beware, Abby. You must be careful not to overdo. Take time to be alone and study your own heart. Then you will succeed."

Miss Louisa put away the cards and patted my cheek.

"Abby will succeed through hard work, not superstition, Miss Adams." It was Doctor, talking in an angry tone.

"Ah, Doctor Howe. The Fate Lady has displeased you again. Is it because you see yourself in Abby's fate?"

"I do not subscribe to such occult nonsense."

"It is said that you labor so hard to secure your school, you take no time to be alone," said Miss Louisa. "Or to need someone else. Don't take your fate out on the child."

I waited for Doctor to bark back at Miss Louisa. But instead he sighed and scooted me off the stool. Then he sat down and put his arm around my shoulders. He said, "I have five dollars left to my name. Deal out your cards for this old bachelor."

"First give me your hand." Miss Louisa and Doctor stayed silent. "Ah, yes," she said. "I feel something already. It is the power, Doctor, of your great heart."

❧   ❧   ❧

The May Fair was over, and so was school, for the summer. It had been exciting to be the center of attention in Boston. And we had learned so much at school, we were almost bursting with ideas and skills. Still, we missed home something awful. We had not been with the family since Christmas. So we wanted to stay—but we wanted to go. We packed our travel boxes in our room.

"Aren't you glad Papa was too busy to drive down for us?" I said to Sophia. "This way we get to be coach travelers."

"No," Sophia grumbled. "We have to spend the whole day bouncing around with strangers. I'll be terrible shy."

She might be right, but I wouldn't admit it. "I always wanted to drive up to our tollhouse," I said. "Mr. Holt will greet us. And the boys will run down from the house."

"Do you imagine we'll get the money for the mansion?" she asked. "So we can have school in September?"

"We surely will," I said. (Didn't the Fate Lady tell me so?) Then a voice called, "It's me, Maria, to say good-bye."

"Come in, Maria," said Sophia. "Are you leaving now?"

"Yes. My parents and brother came to the fair. They are waiting to drive me back to Cambridge. Have a fine summer."

"Thanks, Maria," I said. "We'll miss you."

Maria gave us both a hug. "Practice your knitting. I want to see two perfect pairs of stockings next fall."

"We'll try," I said. "Say, listen! I can hear Doctor's voice. He is coming in with Mr. Mann."

"Abby, can you?" said Sophia. "Let's run down!"

So we all hurried down the staircase. Doctor called his family, us pupils, the Pennimans, and the Bowens into the parlor. "Our head trustee, Mr. Mann, has a report to make," he said.

"The fair was a huge success," Mr. Mann said. "Far beyond our wildest hopes. We have earned almost half our goal! And kindly donors have come forth. They are pledging generous gifts of money."

"But Mann, can we hope to reach our goal by June first?" Doctor asked. "Colonel Perkins won't wait forever."

"I have no doubt of it," said Mr. Mann. "The New England Asylum for the Blind will open on Pearl Street come September."

As Maria and Sophia took my hands, we danced in a circle and the old house shook with the sound of our cheers.

After dinner we were the only pupils remaining. Our coach would leave early in the morning. As we lay in bed, I thought this house had never been home. We were never truly welcomed by its owners. But it would always be where we started our future.

At dawn we waited in the foyer with our travel boxes while Doctor hitched the horse. Cook Sarah and Miss Elizabeth wished us the best of luck, then went back to the pantry to do the marketing list. Mr. Joseph gave us a hearty handshake, then hurried off to his glass factory. The house fell silent. Then a faint weeping sound came from upstairs. Sophia asked, "Where is Miss Jeanette?"

"I think she is too sad to see us leave."

Doctor drove the hackney up the brick path. "Come along, girls," he called. "Let's get to the depot. The stage to Andover won't wait."

As we followed Doctor down the brick path, I stopped and turned. I could not tell if Miss Jeanette—or anyone—was looking out the window. But I waved good-bye.

Down at the depot, Doctor hoisted our travel boxes onto the stage, then gave us each a quick hug. "Remember all you've learned," he said. "God keep you both!"

"And you too, Doctor. Good-bye until fall!"

As we climbed into the coach and got squashed between a big lady and a man who smelled like old cigars, Doctor shouted at the coach driver, "I charge you with these children! They are very young and blind."

The driver's reply was a crack of the whip.

I thought folks would talk about the interesting sights we were passing. All they did was grumble. When it started to rain, the road got muddy and rutted, causing slow travel. These people had traveled before and thought it was an awful burden. At noon the big lady said, "You girls follow me to the Necessary." Then she set us at a planked table in the depot tavern, where we got a mug of milk, a slab of hard cheese on coarse bread, and a dried apple. When I heard the coach driver beside us, I asked, "How much time until Andover, sir?"

"Much as this damnable mud allows," he said. "Don't you trouble the folks in the coach. You hear me?"

"Yes, sir. We hear very well," I said politely.

After lunch, Sophia and I dreamed and dozed as we bumped along. I awoke to a shout: "Andover Toll-house! Toll, please."

It was our friend. "Soph, did you hear Mr. Holt?" I nudged her. "We're home!"

Sophia lifted her head from my shoulder. "We are?"

"Yes! Hey, Mr. Holt, it's us, Abby and Sophia Carter!"

Sophia and I climbed over the big lady, then got swung down by Mr. Holt. The sweet spring smells of the farm greeted us. The soft rain ran down our cloaks and off our noses. "Hello, Mr. Holt," I said. "Where's our papa?"

"He's sent your brothers down the path twice already, looking for you. My, you girls grew some!"

"Yes," said Sophia. "And we can read now, and write our letters, and sing our vocals, and add and subtract!"

"Merciful heaven," said Mr. Holt. "That's mighty

hard to believe. Here come Richard and Justin for you."

Richard and Justin came racing to the tollhouse, panting. "Your coach is late," said Richard.

"We're supposed to carry your travel boxes," said Justin. "Abby, can you still find your way up the path? Or are you just a city girl now?"

I stood there by the tollhouse, feeling turned around. Maybe I was still sleepy from the coach ride—I *didn't* remember the path. I put my hand to my mouth. My fingers had grown delicate from reading the tiny raised letters and numbers. How could I do the summer chores for Mam? Where did I belong?

"Abby, what's the matter?" Sophia groped for my hand.

"We're going on," Richard called as he walked away. "These boxes are too heavy to wait on you."

"Yes, we're coming," I said softly. I turned my face up to heaven. The rain had stopped, and a sweet warm breeze blew from the west. I could smell our cattle, the big pond, the blooming shrubs. Beyond our farm were our neighbors' farms. Some of them had girls who went into town to the Female Academy. When we would all meet at church socials, they never talked much to me. They would talk to each other about what they did at school. But now I had been to school too. Now I was more like them. For the

first time, I was eager to meet them at summer picnics.

I heard the coach driver crack his whip and the horses gallop off, pulling the passengers on to their own stops. And I realized that most people were lucky if they had one home to go to. But Sophia and I had two homes. The home inside our head would always be with Doctor and school. But the home inside our heart would always be with Mam and Papa and the boys here on the farm.

"We don't need the boys to find our way," I told Sophia. "We have the outstretched hand and the slippered foot." Gingerly I started leading her down the path. Soon a squishy wet feeling came through my slipper. I stopped. "I remember the path," I told her. "But I don't remember the puddles!"

Sophia started to giggle. "Me neither. I guess we'll just have to splash right through them."

I laughed along with her as we turned our slippers into muddy waders. We laughed all the way up the path.

15
The Magic Road Goes On

My three girls leaned in as I paused in my story. We were huddled together in my bedroom on Pearl Street in the new Asylum for the Blind.

"What happened then?" Lurena demanded. She had no patience when I paused in my stories.

"Mam was so annoyed with me, because I had lost my hands for farm chores. So she made me do the nastiest job. Plucking."

"What's plucking?" Harriet asked timidly. Harriet was a very sheltered girl. I gathered she'd done little to help at home.

"Plucking? Why, pulling out the feathers of birds to roast. And along with plucking those partridges out by the barn, I had to watch Edward."

My girls knew who Edward was already. I had been telling them a story each evening before bedtime. We had been in the new school for three weeks. Each of the former pupils got to be leaders of three new ones. My girls were lonesome for home. Lurena and Mary were coming along. Harriet was miserable. But my stories helped ease them to dreamland. And Edward, their favorite rascal, played a part in most of my tales.

"How could you watch Edward?" Mary asked. "With both of you being blind . . ."

"It was a trial," I admitted. "Edward knew he was to stay near enough to catch or call. He was making mud birds when I—"

"What's mud birds?" said Harriet.

Use your imagination, I wanted to say. But I explained, "You make a mud ball. Then you find tail feathers from the plucked birds and stick them in. After they dry, you have a toy bird."

"Harriet," said Lurena, "let Abby tell her story."

"I kept plucking in the warm sun," I went on. "And my mind started roaming back here to school. I heard the cows low, and the crows call, and the flies buzz, and Edward chatter to his birds. Then it all blended into a dream. I heard Mr. Trencheri at reading lesson, and scales on the piano, and Miss Jeanette's recess bell. . . . Suddenly the flies bit my hands and I woke up with a yell. Edward! Edward! I patted all around the barn grass. Edward and the mud birds were gone."

"Oh no, didn't he hear you calling?" Lurena said.

"I can't bear it if it's sad!" Mary cried.

Harriet began to sniffle.

I knew that Sophia and her three girls were listening from the doorway. I hoped she would not chime in and ruin the exciting part. "Someone else heard me scream," I said. "It was my brother Richard. I was so scared that Edward had gone back to the big pond. I got turned around and forgot which way to go."

"Of course," said Lurena. "Your parents asked too much of you."

"Please don't tell me Edward drowned!" Mary said.

"Well, Richard came running," I said. "When he heard about Edward, he could make out something moving back by the pond. 'Richard, grab him,' I said, 'or he'll get drowned for sure.' "

Harriet started rocking and sniffling. I pulled her hands away from her ears. "Listen, this is the good part," I said to her. "Richard made a dash for the pond. I vowed I'd never be selfish and daydream if only I could hear Edward whining again."

I paused one more moment before the most exciting part. "And . . . then I did! Richard had him! He was dragging him back!"

"Abby, Edward was saved!" Mary said, and hugged me.

"I hope you thrashed him good," Lurena added.

"I shook him hard and told him never to forget

again that the pond is danger. Richard can't always save us. We blind must learn to save ourselves. And that's why—"

"We can't," Harriet moaned. "People must take care of us."

"And that's why we are at school," I repeated. I liked to bring school in at the end of my stories. "To learn."

"Did you get a punishment from your parents?" Lurena asked.

"I did. Remember, they already lost two sons. One was to an accident. I was mighty ashamed. So I promised . . ."

The bell chimed from down the hall. In our mansion, now changed into a school, we had bells for classes, meals, and bedtimes. We now had almost thirty students and a regular music teacher, along with Mr. Trencheri and Mr. Pringle. Doctor also hired a matron to keep charge of all of us, our laundry and belongings, and a cook. Miss Jeanette came along to live with us and help Doctor. Even in such a big house, we often bumped into each other. Matron called, "Enough, Abby the storyteller. Girls, each one in her bed."

"Good night, Mrs. Moulton," we called back.

As we drifted off to sleep, we heard Harriet's sniffles. I expect she went home in her dreams.

❧   ❧   ❧

Not only did I have to look after Lurena, Mary, and Harriet in our room at night, but I kept track of them during the day. As I said, Lurena and Mary paid attention at lessons and found their way around the school. Harriet stuck to me like a burr. Although she came from the country, she did no chores. Her father kept her in the parlor most days for fear she'd hurt herself. Her life at home was dull, but she missed it. She was slow to learn and babylike. Even little Edward had more spunk than Harriet.

"I can't do it, Abby," she would say each evening. "I can't keep it all in my head. I think about home, and—poof—the lesson is gone."

"Then stop your daydreaming," I told her. "Remember my story about losing Edward?"

"Yes. I'll try, if you help me."

After a month, Doctor told us that two of the new girls had to be sent home. They had a sickness called consumption of the lungs. Doctor could not let a pupil remain who was so sick. Harriet tried coughing and moping like those two girls. Mrs. Moulton told her to stop the foolishness; she was not sick at all. Then one afternoon at recess, Harriet disappeared.

We were never to leave the playground without a guide. So where could Harriet be? I strolled to the back, calling, "Harriet? Did you fall? Where are you?"

Finally I heard a sniffling sound from the back bushes. "Harriet, I hear you. You're supposed to practice strolling with the other girls. You'd better answer me!"

Harriet crawled out and said, "I heard folks walking on the street behind the bushes. I was trying to get them to talk to me." Then she started to cry.

"Now stop that weeping," I said as I pulled her by the arm. "You can talk to everyone at school."

"I was trying to find someone. But they paid me no mind. One child stopped. The mother said, 'Don't go near the idiot girl.' "

"Oh, for heaven's sake. We aren't idiots, Harriet!"

"I just wanted someone to write to Father. Ask him to say he can't do without me. And must fetch me home." She wept again.

I lost my temper. "Harriet, you get to your feet before I pull your hair." Harriet did. As she took my hand, the bell rang. We'd be late to music class, but I had to get her to listen.

"This is our chance to have lessons," I said. "I know they are hard. The words and numbers pound in your head. But you can't live your whole life in your parlor and not learn."

"I belong at home with Father," Harriet insisted.

I knew Harriet's mother was dead. "You want to keep the house for your father? That's good. The more you learn at school, the more help you will be to him. That's why he sent you here."

As Harriet sniffed, I gave her my kerchief. "Remember my stories about the tollhouse?" Harriet said yes. "I found out what was at the end of the turnpike. It's our school. Here our lessons are seeing lessons. After you learn them, you are never truly blind again."

"I'm still frightened, Abby."

"Not with Doctor. He took me and Sophia by the hand. He can lead us all." We were startled to hear large boots crunching the leaves behind us. "Abby. Harriet. You are late for music class."

"Sorry, Doctor."

Doctor took Harriet's hand. She kept stumbling, not having practiced the slippered foot. Doctor never let her fall. When we reached the back porch, Mrs. Moulton called, "Ah, the lost ducklings."

"Harriet, follow Mrs. Moulton to the music room. I must have a talk with Abby." Doctor sat me down beside him on the steps. I wondered if he would give me a punishment for being late. "It's been a busy day," he said. "Let's rest a minute."

Rest? The Doctor never took a rest. "Abby," he said, "I listened in on you girls. About Harriet's fears."

Doctor had played the spy? I smiled to recall how I had done it to him on our first day at school. "Harriet wants her father to fetch her home," I said. "She was going to try a trick. . . ."

"I have known all along that school was a big leap for Harriet. She is a burden for you. But you were the only one to help her take that first step."

"Do you think Harriet will stay here?"

"I hope so. For some blind, that trip down the road from home is so very frightening."

"Doctor, sometimes the trip back home is hard too. I missed school so much over the summer. Sometimes that got me into trouble. I didn't know where I belonged."

Doctor patted my shoulder. "Thank you for telling me that. It takes a lifetime to find where you belong, if you are in some way different. Like we are."

"Different but special," I whispered. "Like a black swan."

"Where did you hear of a black swan? My mother used to call me that."

The sounds of piano and singing lessons floated down the hall. Doctor rose and took my hand. I never spoke to him again about the black swan. And I decided at that moment I would somehow keep Harriet in school. "We won't give up on Harriet, will we?"

"Give up?" Doctor stopped and said firmly, "Abby Carter, those are two words we never use. Off to class you go."

I hurried down the hall, eager to be part of the music.

Afterword

Abby Carter was never one to "give up." She became one of the best students at what was later called the Perkins Institution for the Blind. She and Sophia helped Dr. Howe in many ways. They found the courage to speak out for the blind at state legislatures. They traveled with Dr. Howe all the way to the territory called the Ohio Frontier. They urged people to start their own schools for the blind. They assisted the younger pupils at the institution, one of whom was named Laura Bridgman. This girl was the first American child who was both deaf and blind to be educated. Laura's special friendship with the Carter sisters helped her survive.

Abby, we are told in a memoir by her little sister Emily Carter, lived a rich life as a musician and teacher. She worked and taught at the Perkins Institution until 1842. As a young woman, she returned to Andover, helped her parents at home, and taught vocal and instrumental music. She taught private pupils from several towns and also taught classes at schools for young ladies. Abby was so admired by the adults in her town that she formed evening vocal classes just for them. Active in her church, Abby wrote beautiful religious poems and hymns. Although illness struck her, she taught almost to the day of her death in April 1875.

Sophia also had a career in music. She earned her living teaching singing at the Perkins Institution. She worked as a soloist in Boston churches. Later in her life she returned to Andover. Along with Abby, she helped take care of her younger siblings, William, Emily, and Albert. Their mother had died in 1845. Those early lessons in knitting, handiwork, and crocheting paid off for Sophia. Her work was always in demand and gave her a good income. Until she died in October 1888, Sophia was a busy, beloved member of her community.

Records at Perkins tell us that Benjamin Bowen graduated, married, and taught school for the blind in Louisville, Kentucky. Joseph Smith graduated, went on to study at Harvard University, and taught. Charles Morrill played piano, organ, and violin; married; and taught to support his family. Maria Penniman returned to Cambridge to keep house. All these young people became active citizens. Dr. Howe's dream for them came true.

The Perkins Institution for the Blind grew and grew. When the number of pupils rose to sixty-five, Dr. Howe could not house them in the mansion on Pearl Street. The school moved to a former hotel in South Boston. Dr. Howe kept an apartment there, married Julia Ward, and had a family of six children. Sadly, Samuel and Julia lost their youngest boy to childhood illness. But the other five Howes grew up to be teachers, writers, and scientists.

Dr. Howe's accomplishments would take another book to list. He continued to direct the school until he died in 1876. The Howe Press published many books in English for the blind. Dr. Howe also started the first school for young people with mental retardation. During the Civil War, Dr. Howe was appointed to inspect sanitary conditions at Union Army Hospitals. While riding with him, Julia Ward Howe was moved to write "The Battle Hymn of the Republic."

Dr. Howe always regarded the pupils of the Perkins Institution as his own family. When writing to a friend in 1835, he was still unmarried. He wrote: "I am a bachelor, but no, I have children—five & forty children—for the pupils of the Institution under my charge are, and ought to be, like children to me." The graduates of the Perkins Institution felt the same way about him. Many believed that although their own fathers gave them birth, Dr. Howe gave them a life.

Perkins House

Colonel Thomas Perkins